What the shift?

Contents

Chapter One

Faelynn

What's worse than running down a creepy, deserted street in a ballgown? Running barefoot in a ballgown, that's what. I ditched my heels three blocks back and already regret it. Not because it was easier to run, but because the gods only knew what I was stepping in. The squelch between my toes proved my point and I prayed that it wasn't something I couldn't wash off, like gum.

Fighting the urge to gag, I returned my focus to the street in front of me. I squinted in the dark so I wouldn't accidentally trip or step in anything else. The sound of pursuing footsteps pounded in my ears but I was half convinced it was my heart that I was hearing.

I darted around a corner entering a street that I didn't recognize. The sidewalk was old and crumbling, small chips of concrete poking the soles of my feet as I ran.

The street took a sharp left turn so I hurried around it, hoping my pursuers weren't that close behind me.

The evening had gone to hell faster than I could comprehend.

The annual Gala was an event that all shifters were encouraged to attend. It was a time for the packs to get together, mates to be found, and bargains to strike. Most looked forward to this annual party, especially the higher echelon who treated this as a time to show off and one up each other.

My pack was no different and while I appreciated the Gala for what it was, I also resented it.

As the youngest daughter to the alpha of the Aruna pack, I was sought after for my position and genetics. A female born to an alpha line would surely produce strong alpha children, so naturally I was to be auctioned off like cattle to the highest bidder.

That's not the reason I was running through the dark city streets when I could be dancing and sipping champagne. Nope. I'd snuck away from the Gala and found my secluded nook that was tucked behind a bookcase. I grabbed a book then settled in to read the rest of the night away, chuckling when I thought of my suitors frantically looking for me.

I was engrossed in the angsty romance between the two lead characters when the sound of voices interrupted my reading. I drew further into the corner, tucking the fabric of my dress around my legs.

"How could you have lost her?" an angry voice growled. I gulped, wishing the floor would open up and swallow me so I wouldn't be eavesdropping.

"She was there, then the next second, gone." an even angrier voice growled back and I flinched when I recognized the voice as Candri.

Candri was the alpha apparent to the Apollo pack which had the largest number of shifters. The name also meant 'wolf king' and the bastard had taken it to heart, letting his ego grow wild with it.

"I told you to watch her closely." the first voice snarled and my brows drew together because it sounded like Chantara. "She always sneaks off during the Gala and isn't seen again for hours. Thanks to you, we probably won't see her until it's time to go."

"We'll find her," Candri said, his voice deepening seductively and I fought the urge to barf.

"You better!" Chantara exclaimed, followed by the sound of ripping fabric. "On your knees."

The order was strange and so unlike the soft-spoken girl who I counted as a friend but now I wasn't so sure.

Rumbles, grunts, sighs, and moans followed the order and I was tempted to peek but I also didn't want to add naked flesh to my nightmares. I hoped that once they were done they would speak more about what they wanted with me.

Sneaking off to have sex at the Gala was normal. Shifters, especially wolves, were affectionate creatures and needed physical touch. I'd had such relations before, most were disappointing. There was only one who hadn't been but he'd disappeared and hadn't been seen since.

"You're sure about her?" Candri asked, his voice startling me back to awareness.

"Yes. I've seen it myself," Chantara said, clearly annoyed. "She has a silver patch on her thigh when she shifts. It's hard to tell because she is a white wolf but I've seen it shimmer in the moonlight."

I had to hold in my gasp as I realized they were talking about me. The birthmark on my thigh grew silver fur when I shifted but only a select few people knew about it. My father had always acted weird about it but refused to say why. At the Gala five years ago I snooped through the archives and found a legend about silver fur. It said that a wolf with a spot of silver was blessed by the Moon Spirit and from that line would rise an Alpha Seeker.

Whatever that was.

I'd found it in a book of pup stories so I didn't believe it was anything concerning or that it pertained to me in any way.

"The ritual is ready. All we need is her blood and your seed." Chantara spoke with excitement and it hurt my heart.

"It'll work," Candri announced with confidence and the rustling told me they were getting dressed again. "The Alpha Seeker will come from my line."

Screw that.

Candri was insufferable, cruel, and disgusting. Just thinking of him touching me was enough to make my heart race and bile to coat my throat. Were they talking about sex?

My blood and his seed?

They needed to hurry up and leave so I could get out of there. I'm not sure where I'd go, to my father probably but he was probably balls deep in some hussy, praying for another boy.

No, what I needed to do was figure out what this ritual was and how to stop it. Having silver fur couldn't be that uncommon since we were technically all the Moon Spirit's children. Why was a silver patch so important?

The murmur of their voices echoed through the space as the door clicked shut behind them. I waited as long as I dared before rising tentatively from the floor, my dress tangled around my legs.

I looked around making sure the room was empty before venturing out. My best bet for information was the archives but I hadn't been in there in years. The last time had left me panting, sore, and ruined.

The archives were on this floor but at the end of the hallway. I'd need to traverse the open area without being seen but with people looking it will be harder. My heels and dress didn't help with stealthiness so I'd have to be careful.

I opened the door enough so I could see down the hallway. It was deserted but that didn't mean anything to shifters. I scented the air then wrinkled my nose as the smell of sex overpowered the area.

Gross.

I slipped out of the room and tiptoed down the hallway, the fabric of my blue dress in my hands. The thought of my dress and the meaning behind it struck me as funny now. A blue dress with sparkly white fabric to represent moonlight because "once in a blue moon".

Having a dress made for a theme only I knew about was humorous and I suppose a slap in the face to the Gala's theme. Not that I cared.

A few more steps and then I could slip into the archives unseen. The prospect of actually sneaking in unnoticed was exhilarating.

"That's her!" A voice yelled and I turned to see three male shifters wearing the colors of Apollo entering the other end of the hallway.

"Shit!" I grumbled, abandoning my goal and instead opening the door on the left revealing a staircase.

I slipped in then closed the door, flipping the lock, hoping that would slow them down enough that I could escape.

I tapped into my wolf's stamina and balance and all but flew down the three flights of stairs. At the ground floor I heard the door open and the yells of the Apollo guards from above.

Pushing the doors to the outside open I didn't bother to try to lock them, instead putting all my energy and concentration into running in heels.

This is stupid.' My inner wolf grumbled, speaking up for the first time as I crossed the street.

'Yes, well Candri fucking us wasn't something I wanted to stick around for.' I huffed, focusing on not twisting an ankle.

'Oh yeah, fuck that guy!' She agreed, lending me her strength and agility. *'You should ditch the heels.'*

After three blocks I took a moment to slip my strappy heels off and tossed them into a dumpster.

Now for speed.

Three blocks later I was huffing and cringing at what my feet could be stepping in. I ducked around a corner and sprinted down the sidewalk as my path veered to the left.

As the end of the street came into view I realized it was a dead end.

Damnit.

A golden light shone into the street mixing with the moonlight and shadows. I squinted my eyes and found that it was a bookstore. The sign above the door said, 'Book's End.' A weird place for a bookstore, down a secluded street and open at odd hours.

Making a quick decision, I hurried to the door, still astonished that there was an open sign in the window. I grabbed the stupid bell so it wouldn't chime as I opened the door and closed it quietly.

The store was empty. And quiet.

A 'U' shaped checkout counter was placed against the wall on the left side. I looked around but didn't find a suitable hiding place, so the counter, it was.

I hurried around it, noticing a hoodie conveniently placed over a stool. I snatched it and grabbed a pair of black rimmed glasses from a display.

With only seconds to decide I quickly unzipped my dress and stepped out of it. I then stuffed it under the counter between a trash can and a computer tower. Pulling the hoodie on I let it drop over my torso then pulled the hood up, hiding my nearly white hair. I shoved the glasses onto my face then grabbed a book from a stack on the counter and began reading.

My heart pounded in my chest as my eyes tried to focus on the book and not on my pursuers. The fan at the end of the counter moved and blew my way and I choked on a gasp when I felt the cool air blow across my exposed backside.

Shit! Of all nights to wear a thong.

The little bell jingled on the door, turning my attention to the front of the shop. The three Apollo guards entered the shop looking around at the empty shop.

"Can I help you?" I asked the trio of guards very aware of my ass hanging out.

"Have you seen a young lady in a blue dress?" The lead wolf asked, or rather, demanded.

"Uh, no." I responded, looking around the empty shop while also nudging my dress with my foot.

"Do you mind if we have a look around?"

"No, by all means." I said, gesturing to the rest of the shop.

I adjusted my glasses then leaned over my book putting my ass on display. Thank goodness there wasn't a mirror behind me.

The guards shuffled around the place searching for me when it was all I could do to not fidget and draw attention to my nearly naked backside.

"I don't smell anything," one of the guards whispered and my heart clenched like a hand had wrapped around it but before I could panic a throat cleared.

All the guards whipped around to face the newcomer including me though I belatedly tried to make it look like it wasn't a total surprise.

A shifter stood next to an open door that I hadn't noticed before. He wore pants, had a slim waist and broad shoulders. Oh, and he was shirtless and sweaty like he'd just been working out.

Tattoos rolled over his muscled skin and I followed them with my eyes as they dipped and twisted. My thighs clenched as I took in the Adonis that stood only a few feet away. A drop of sweat ran down his shoulder and I fought the urge to lick it off his golden skin.

"Have you seen a girl in a blue ballgown and heels?" The lead guard asked the man which shook me from my staring.

My eyes wandered to his face and found that his seafoam green eyes were transfixed on my exposed ass. I wanted to slap my forehead but I had to act like seeing a shirtless man in an empty bookstore was normal.

"No," the man said, his deep voice and eyes reminding me of someone.

Just then his eyes flicked up to mine and I had to stifle another gasp or maybe a moan. What were the odds I'd run into the very man who'd once satisfied me so fully that I was now ruined for any other in a deserted bookstore?

I'm shit at math.

Chapter Two

R aff

The bell on the door drew my attention so I put the weights down, grabbing my towel to wipe my face while trying to remember if I locked the door or flipped the sign to close. Damn, I don't remember turning off the lights either.

The Gala always fucked with my head so instead I was working my muscles until they screamed.

I tossed the towel into the hamper and made my way toward the door that led to the store front. I could hear scuffing coming from the other side and I gritted my teeth ready to rip the thief apart.

I swung the door open wide then strolled into the store, muscles bulging as I looked around for the idiots who entered a shop in the middle of the night.

My feet stopped in their tracks then rooted to the floor and I took in the incredible backside currently bent over the counter. My cock twitched as I took in the rounded flesh on display. The thin piece of fabric that ran between them then around her hips made my balls ache.

"I don't smell anything." A gruff voice said, his tone suspicious.

That got my attention but not enough to pull my eyes from the creamy skin and legs. I cleared my throat, letting the easy smirk I'd perfected to tilt one side of my mouth.

Four sets shifter eyes flicked to me but I ignored all of them except the stunning blue ones. They looked me up and down and I felt my muscles tense unconsciously as she looked me over. I felt her gaze like a caress on my skin and damn if it didn't heat my blood.

"Have you seen a girl in a blue ball gown and heels?" A male voice asked and I was instantly annoyed.

"No." I nearly growled ignoring the blue fabric that was stuffed under the counter though the glasses held me transfixed for several seconds.

When Faelynn's eyes flicked up to mine I saw surprise and lust in their depths that made my wolf howl in my head.

"You sure?" A different guard said and my focus snapped to him and for the first time I noticed the colors he wore.

Apollo.

The fucking pack who'd gotten me exiled from the Gala and all joint pack meetings. A snarl built in my throat and I debated giving in and letting my wolf tear them apart. Before I could, the slight gasp and elevated heartbeat from Faelynn told me she was scared.

I paused thinking it was me who she was frightened of but then her eyes flicked to the three Apollos then adjusted her hood. It clicked, they were searching for her.

But why?

Faelynn was Aruna so had no business with Apollo unless that fuckwit Candri had won her hand but I would have heard about it. Whatever the case, she was running from them which was reason enough for me to protect her.

"Did I fucking stutter?" I asked dangerously, unable to keep the bite from my wolf out of my voice.

They all drew back at my hostility which was good. My dominance ran deep and my wolf and I wouldn't stand for them disrespecting us or her.

I walked around the counter, putting it between me and the Apollo wolves so I wouldn't be tempted to maul them. Faelynn stood frozen, her bare legs just begging to be touched while the sight of her in my hoody made me want to pound my chest like some neanderthal.

I wrapped my arm around her waist, pulling her close as I glared at the trespassing wolves, a clear challenge in my eyes.

No one moved, though I was acutely aware of Faelynn's frantic heart racing and her quick breaths.

"It's Gala night." I told them, raising my eyebrows at them.

10

They all smirked then nodded before turning and walked toward the door.

"Sorry to have bothered you." The lead wolf apologized, then left the door to swing shut.

I dropped my hand and went to the door, locking it. I turned the sign over then closed the window shade and turned off the light.

Turning I saw that Faelynn was in the same position, her mouth agape as she once again studied my naked chest. My thigh muscles clenched as I took her in, wanting to wrap her in my arms and breathe in her scent.

I was around the counter again, crowding her with my body. She leaned back against the counter pupils dilated and chest rising and falling with her erratic breathing. After all these years I still had an effect on her as she did me.

"Raff?" She asked, my name on her lips had my ab muscles spasming as the urge to take her was almost too much for me to fight.

"Faelynn." I responded, my voice rumbling huskily as I leaned closer, our chests nearly touching.

I breathed in her scent, agreeing with my wolf when he growled possessively and it took every ounce of will I could muster not to touch her.

Not yet.

Her palm touched my cheek, startling me as did the tears gathering in her eyes. "I thought you were dead."

"What?" My eyes widened in astonishment followed swiftly by anger. "Who told you I was dead?"

"No one I just assumed…" She trailed off, her earlier annoyance was replaced with something else. "If you're not dead then where have you been all this time?"

"I've been in exile." I said, my brows furrowing as the truth hit me like a load of bricks. "No one told you."

"Told me what?" She huffed, angrily.

"Five years ago when we snuck into the archives…"

"What about it?" She crossed her arms over her chest and I realized that it wasn't just anger she was feeling but hurt.

"It's forbidden. They found my scent and confronted me about it. I convinced them I'd acted alone." I revealed, looking down at her surprised face, my anger rising again.

"So they exiled you?" She whispered, looking shocked.

"For five years. That was my sentence." I told her keeping the part that having her safe was worth the punishment.

"Oh Gods!" She exclaimed, covering her mouth with her hand, tears leaking from her eyes. "I thought it was me. That you'd changed your mind."

"No." I couldn't stand it any longer, I grabbed her and pulled her against me. My hand cupped the back of her head as she cried into my chest.

My wolf grumbled with annoyance but also contentment. It had been so long since we held her, touched her, scented her. Just her nearness was driving my wolf half crazed with lust and desire.

"I waited for you." She sniffled and my heart clenched. Of course she did. She'd promised to and so had I then when I didn't show up...

My hands tightened, gripping her with almost bruising force as she cried out her anger and hurt.

"I'm sorry." The words felt hollow when I said them but the conviction behind them was staggering.

Her hands slid down my back, the feeling going straight to my cock like she was stroking it instead of my back.

"Raff?" She asked, her head leaning back so she could see my face.

"Hmmm?" I hummed my response, my eyes roaming her face telling myself that this wasn't a dream.

Her eyes flicked down to my lips before she rose on tiptoe and pressed her lips to mine. She wrapped her arms around my neck while I pressed her against the counter. My chest vibrated as her taste exploded on my tongue.

My hands slid down her thighs, gripping them as I lifted her onto the counter. I devoured her mouth, my tongue plundering as my fingers dug into her thighs.

She spread her legs, allowing me to wedge my hips between them. Faelynn moaned when my hands slid under the hem of the hoodie.

"Raff." She sighed, as my lips and tongue moved to her throat.

She leaned her head back, eyes closed in obvious rapture as I kissed and tasted her skin. A growl built in my throat at her submissive and my mouth water as the urge to bite her, to claim her overtook me.

I pushed back, away from her, having to bodily rip my wolf away. I wrestled with him for control for what felt like an eternity.

"Raff?" Faelynn asked, her sweet voice a balm to the ragged edges of my control.

"I'm sorry." My voice was deeper than normal, my wolf close to the surface wanting to touch her as much as I did.

"Did you almost lose control?" She asked, and I nodded my head ashamed at my lack of control around her. "Me too."

Her words made my eyes jerk up to her face and I saw the seriousness written all over her beautiful features.

"I nearly lost control five years ago and again just now."

She swallowed and my body jerked forward, the urge to run my teeth along the delicate column of her throat almost too much for me to fight.

"Your wolf doesn't want to rip my throat out does he?" Faelynn asked, and the question made my gut clench. "I'm kidding. It was either that or claiming and your expression answered the question."

"We'd never hurt you." My wolf and I said the different inflections making it impossible to lie.

"But you'd claim me?" One of her eyebrows rose in question and I fought a smirk at her challenge.

"My wolf would have claimed you five years ago if I'd let him." I revealed, watching her closely to see how my words would affect her view of me.

"Why didn't you?" She asked, the question taking me by surprise.

"Would you have wanted me too? Take away your choices without your family's blessing?" I couldn't ask her to do that not then and definitely not now.

"But if you'd asked me first," she took a step closer and my eyes were drawn to her hands fidgeting with the hem of the hoody.

"Asked?" I swallowed, wondering why I hadn't and what she would have said if I did.

"Yeah, why didn't you ask?" She wondered, bright eyes fixed on my face.

A shiver of nervousness raced down my spine. She wasn't just challenging my words but also my actions. It made me want to kiss and smack her ass all at the same time.

"I guess...I couldn't handle the rejection." I answered, truthfully.

"I wouldn't have rejected you." She whispered, taking another step closer, her chin tilting so her eyes could meet mine. "Ask me."

My heart stuttered in my chest while my cock jumped to attention.

She was telling me to ask her and while my wolf was urging me to do just that I couldn't help but feel like I was standing on a landmine.

Chapter Three

Faelynn

Raff looked like a deer caught in headlights, or in this case a wolf. Challenging him had always been fun because it seemed like I was the only one who could surprise him.

I might have gone a little too far telling him to ask me right now. Was he ready? Was I? Usually matings had fanfare not to mention the bargaining beforehand where our families would each get something.

Asking him to ask me took all of that away and it was…exhilarating. Why couldn't we mate because we wanted to? Matings were always political when it came to the alpha families. A subject I hated because it meant I had no control, no choice, no say in any of it.

That didn't sit well with my wolf who was as dominant as any alpha but my lack of a cock meant I had no say.

"Faelynn…" Raff began then paused and my heart sank.

He wasn't going to ask me, he'd make up some lame excuse and probably escort me home. That was the last thing I wanted.

Now that I knew he wasn't dead but alive this whole time, it made my heart spasm in my chest. We'd known of each other all our lives but our first meeting was at the Gala five years ago. That night changed and ruined me all at the same time. No one else could compare to him and I'd tried to banish his memory but I couldn't.

17

"Faelynn?" Raff asked, pulling my attention back to the present and I realized he'd asked me something.

"Hmm, sorry. What did you say?"

"Will you mate with me?" The question took me by surprise rendering me speechless.

He'd asked.

He'd asked and here I was staring up at him like an idiot. I opened my mouth to ask if he was fucking serious but I could tell he was from the rigidness of his shoulders and the set of his jaw.

"Yes," I breathed, barely able to believe that he'd mustered up the courage to ask me.

I was swept against him the next second, my legs wrapping around his hips as he returned me to the counter. His lips caught mine in a kiss that scorched and had me seeing stars.

I ran my hands over his chest and shoulders then lower over his abs. His muscles jumped and twitched under my hands, their hardness making me want to lick every one of them.

His hands were under the hoodie, his fingers caressing my skin as he lifted the fabric up over my head. My hands grabbed his neck pulling his face back down to mine.

A moan sounded from my throat as his tongue plundered my mouth while his hands ran over my skin. I grabbed his hips and pulled him into me, enjoying his grunt when my hands moved to the waistband of his sweatpants.

He growled, his chest vibrating against me as he took over removing every scrap of fabric between us.

I broke the kiss needing to catch my breath and touch every part of him that I could reach. My hand found his cock. It was harder than any other I'd touched and it made me smile knowing that this was how I affected him.

His mouth moved to my chest. Hands cupping my full breasts made me groan as he explored.

It had been five years since we'd done this and yet it felt like yesterday. I ran my teeth over his collarbone feeling powerful as he shivered and his cock jumped in my hand.

I cried out when his hand touched the junction of my thighs. He groaned when he felt how wet, hot, and ready I was. My nails dug into his shoulders as he positioned himself at my entrance.

Bright green eyes met mine and remained there as he slowly pushed into me. I gasped, the feeling of him stretching me also as good as the orgasm that was soon to follow.

"Yes, Raff!" I encouraged as he continued to push into me, his length and girth making tears spring to my eyes.

The invasion was exquisite and I held onto his shoulders until he'd fully seated himself inside me.

"Fuck!" He growled, his hands gripping my ass as he stilled.

I whimpered, needing movement or friction, not above begging for it if I had to.

Raff's chest was heaving and I watched him battle for control while silently wishing he'd just let go.

"Shhhh," I cooed next to his ear hoping to help him gain control.

He growled in response but I think it was more towards his wolf than me. He was struggling internally and it had me worried.

"What's wrong?" I asked him cupping his cheek to gain his attention.

"We're disagreeing on whether we should fuck you first then bite you or bite you now then fuck you," Raff answered, his voice deeper than normal.

"Fucking. Please," I begged, trying to move my hips but his hold on me prevented it.

"Fine. We'll fuck you but I'm going to make you come five times, one for each year we were apart." He punctuated his words with small thrusts of his hips that weren't nearly enough.

I whimpered again, biting my lip as he continued the slow torture that was building into something more. My head fell back and I relaxed, letting the slow build of pleasure sweep through me, enjoying every second.

I opened my eyes, still unable to fully believe that Raff was alive and inside me again. Seeing his sea green eyes watching my face was enough to push me over the edge.

My muscles tightened and wave after wave of pleasure swept through my body. I moaned, surprised that the slow build had made me orgasm in less than a minute. Raff's self-satisfied grin made me bite my cheek.

"Five years since I've been inside you," Raff said, running his tongue up the column of my throat, his rock-hard cock still inside me. "Has anyone else fucked you?"

"Yes, but they could never...satisfy me," I replied, truthfully. It was true I'd tried several lovers but he'd ruined me five years ago.

A growl vibrated his chest at the thought of anyone else fucking me and it sent a thrill of excitement through me. Before I could say anything, Raff's hand slipped to the back of my head, fingers spearing through the strands before it tightened into a fist, pulling my head back.

"This is mine," Raff snarled, his wolf fully in control which had my wolf pushing to the surface.

Raff thrust into me, hard. My wolf snarled at the twinge of pain while I moaned as he stretched my tight muscles.

"You ruined us five years ago!" My wolf said using my voice, the hurt in her tone evident.

"It wasn't our fault. To protect you we had to be exiled and we'd do it again to keep you safe." Raff's wolf tried to explain but my wolf was having none of it.

"We can take care of ourself," My wolf retorted, not fazed by the grueling pounding we were taking. My wolf had a bone to pick with Raff's wolf, probably best to let them have it out.

"You're mine!" Raff's wolf growled, continuing to thrust with abandon while still able to hold a conversation. "We protect you. We fuck you. We love and respect you. That's our right."

"As it is our right to do the same for you," my wolf spoke softly, obviously still hurt from her years without him.

The thrusting slowed as Raff's wolf realized how much his absence had hurt us.

"I'm sorry. We were forbidden to contact you. Our sentence would have been extended if we attempted it."

"By whose ruling?" my wolf wondered, our canines tingling with the thought of sinking our teeth into the flesh of someone who's wronged us.

"All the pack alphas were in agreement but it was Apollo who forbade us from contacting you," Raff revealed, and I gasped as my wolf receded enough that we could both feel the crashing orgasm that gripped us.

Even pissed at them they could still please us like no one else ever could. Not even us.

Raff picked me up, cradling me against his broad chest as he walked around the counter and out into the bookstore.

"That's two," Raff said, sitting down on the couch with me straddling him, still incredibly hard.

"How can you keep it up?" I asked, practically boneless after two amazing orgasms.

"I've waited five years to be inside you again. I also promised you an orgasm for every year. I don't break my promises," Raff said, hands lifting my hips so he could start thrusting again.

I pressed my lips to his, dipping my tongue into his mouth. I'd missed the taste of him. He's bigger now, broader in the shoulders and hips, not to mention his thighs, but he was still the wolf I fell in love with and dreamed of mating.

My hips rolled forward, pushing his cock into me at a different angle that made us both gasp. Being on top wasn't my favorite position but I'd gotten in some good practice when the only way I could get off was on top. I used his shoulders for leverage as I basically fucked myself with his cock.

"Your wolf said we ruined you five years ago," Raff breathed, his hands squeezing my hips as I rode him. "You ruined us too."

His words were spoken in the dual tones of him and his wolf. Knowing he was telling the truth and the realization that I meant just as much to him as he did to me threw me into another orgasm. I spasmed around him, groaning as I continued to move to prolong my pleasure.

"Fuck. Raff." I grabbed his neck using it to hold myself up. "I don't think I have anymore in me."

"I think you do." He stood up quickly then laid me down on a cool surface that could only be a coffee table. "Again!"

He drove into me, making me cry out as when the aggressive thrust hit my sensitive walls.

"Fuck." I moaned, feeling his fingers on my clit applying pressure as he drove into me.

"Come on. Come on!" Raff growled, continuing to thrust into me hard while he applied pressure to my clit.

"I can't." I shook my head, unable to take the sensations he was applying.

"Yes you can," he encouraged, gritting his teeth then picking up his rhythm until I was yelling with each thrust.

I yelled, as another orgasm forced my muscles to tense then release in waves of pleasure that were on this side of painful.

"That's four," he said triumphantly, a satisfied smirk on his face.

"I need a break." I tried to catch my breath, but I felt like I was floating on a cloud.

"My balls are turning blue," Raff chuckled, but the look of pain on his face was worrisome.

"I don't know if I can orgasm again." He was still rock hard inside me and I felt closer to him than I ever did to anyone else before.

His hand smoothed my hair back away from my face while his eyes studied every aspect of my features like he was trying to memorize them.

My heart sank.

Chapter Four

Raff

The dreamy look in Faelynn's blue eyes faded and was then replaced by something else.

"What are you thinking?" I asked her, my gut clenching as I watched her.

"Are we still doing this?" She asked instead, searching my eyes for something.

"Mating or sex?" I wondered for clarity while my wolf kept a vice-like grip on my balls.

"Mating," she answered as pain entered her eyes, which made my wolf growl.

"If you still want to," I said slowly. Something had changed over the last minute and I wasn't sure what it was.

"Yes I do, but do you?"

"My decision hasn't changed." I couldn't stop the growl or the thrust that punctuated my words. "You *will* be mine," my wolf added using both of our voices.

"I thought you'd changed your mind," she said, her lip trembling, the emotional movement tugging at my heart.

I shook my head going over everything that I'd said over the past couple minutes, trying to find the mistake.

Her hand cupped my cheek drawing my attention to her face, my eyes searched hers for any hesitation. All I saw was desire, adoration, awe, and underneath all of that, love.

Mine!

Her eyes started to glow as her wolf pushed forward so she could be part of this. I felt my own wolf, silent but a stoic presence, also rise to the surface. No way was he sitting this one out.

I leaned down, running my nose from her collarbone and up her neck. She shivered under me, tilting her chin up and her head to the side, exposing the sensitive flesh of her throat. My balls tightened as my canines descended, my mouth watered at the thought of putting my bite on her skin.

Her back arched, breasts pushing into my chest like she was trying to get closer to me. My chest vibrated as a growl rumbled deep down.

I moved my hips, slowly withdrawing then pushing back in. Faelynn moaned in my ear and I fought the urge to quicken my pace. I'd been fucking her before but now it was different. I wanted to love her this time, show her with my body just how much she meant to me. Even after all these years. She was under my skin and I couldn't wait to have her in every way.

Her hands gripped the skin of my back, nails biting into my muscles which caused an involuntary groan.

"Make me yours," she demanded, her nails growing sharper as my jaw stretched.

My human brain brought forward all of my shortcomings and all the reasons why I could never be what she would want. My wolf pushed everything aside, assuring me that we would be exactly what she needed. We'd love her and do everything we needed to provide for and protect her.

"Mine," my wolf and I said at the same time while my hips sped up.

Faelynn's claws sank into my skin causing me to growl and lean my mouth over her shoulder, saliva pooling in my mouth.

Not like this.

I agreed with my wolf, this wasn't right.

Faelynn yelled when I pulled out of her, making noises of protest when I pulled her to her feet and spun her around. I bent her over the couch, her ass was so inviting that I couldn't help but caress it.

"Raff," Faelynn groaned, the sound alone making my dick leak and my wolf tighten his hold on my balls.

I thrust into her again, a shiver skating down my spine as she adjusted to the new position. My arms wrapped around her, my hand unconsciously finding its way to her throat.

I tilted her head to the side so her throat and collarbone were exposed to me. My wolf rumbled in my chest as I ran my nose up her neck, breathing in her scent, imprinting it in my soul.

"Faelynn." Her name on my tongue was like honey. Sweet with an underlying hint of spice that made my wolf ravenous.

"Fuck me, Raff," she said, her nails digging into the skin of my arm.

"No!" I snarled in her ear, thrusting into her, hard. Her gasp of surprise made me growl in satisfaction. "I'm not going to fuck you. I'm going to fucking love you then I'm going to bite you."

"Yes," she encouraged, pushing her hips back into mine, my cock sliding deeper.

"I've thought of no one else for five years," I said, thrusting into her with a grueling rhythm that verged on pain. "I couldn't stop thinking about you. Your scent, your taste, the way you said my name. I've dreamed of this."

Faelynn's chest was heaving as she yelled with every thrust. I gritted my teeth feeling her tighten around me, so close. My arm muscles tensed around her and I feared I'd hurt her with my relentless pace.

Now!

My teeth sank into the skin where her shoulder meets her neck. Her blood pooled in my mouth, I groaned as her taste and scent overwhelmed my senses.

She gasped at my bite but then turned her head and sank her teeth into my forearm. A roar built in my throat but I swallowed it as she spasmed around me, wringing it so tight that I came, while my dick shuddered inside her.

I felt her swallow then my wolf spirit surged to the forefront of my mind. My consciousness reached for hers and found that she was reaching for me too.

'Faelynn?' I pushed the thought toward her as I licked her bite wound.

'Raff,' her sweet voice in my mind made my knees weak.

I couldn't believe that this was real, that she was mine. My eyes closed and I sent a silent thank you to the Moon Spirit for gifting me the other half of my soul.

"Oh Raff," Faelynn sighed, her body relaxing against mine.

'I've got you, love,' I whispered in her mind then swung her up into my arms.

She was limp in my arms, but if I hadn't known the mate bond would affect her differently I'd be worried. I carried her naked through the bookstore then through my downstairs gym until I reached the stairs that led to my loft.

Walking up the stairs to the place I'd been exiled in was both a nightmare and a dream. This place had been my prison but bringing my blue moon, my mate, nestled securely in my arms was a dream come true.

'Raff,' my name circulated in her thoughts dreamily, and it made my chest ache.

I kicked the door to my room open. The messy bed made me flinch but I set her in the middle of it. A smile spread across my face when hers immediately turned to the pillow I used the most. She was already drawn to my scent like I was to hers.

The thought of her scent in my prison bed made a growl work its way through my body. She deserved a grand bed with silk sheets, only the finest should caress her skin and I vowed that I'd do whatever I could to give her the best of everything.

I crawled into bed, marveling at her immediate movement to my side. Newly mated wolves needed touch or the bond wouldn't solidify. I wrapped my arms around her, unable to think of a single thing that could make me leave this room.

Chapter Five

Faelynn

I snuggled closer to the warmth against my side, a delicious scent filling my nose. There was an underlying smell of sex but it was mostly hidden. The scent jogged my memory and the night before came flooding back.

Fleeing the Gala was pushed aside when I remembered who I'd found in the strangely hidden book shop.

My eyes blinked open and I came face to face with the dream I'd had for years. Raff's face was older now but still breathtakingly handsome. Stubble darkened his jaw while the early morning sun hit his light brown hair, making it brighter until it nearly glowed.

Raff took my breath away just like the first time I saw him.

The room was full of shifters and I was giddy about the prospect of mingling. Being the youngest daughter of the Aruna pack alpha was a title that most wouldn't take lightly. I didn't because I'd been sheltered my whole life, kept out of the public eye. Until tonight.

Attending your first Gala at the age of eighteen was a rite of passage. It was a night to experience many firsts like trying alcohol, experiencing your first kiss, going all the way, or even finding your mate. That last one was a stretch since mates for the elite were chosen instead of found. It was possible but I wasn't holding my breath.

The truth was I was excited to mingle, to be seen and noticed then slip away. The other alpha-daughters were excited to make an impression to garner a suitable match while I had a different objective.

I'd heard whispers my whole life about the silver mark on my wolf's rear left thigh. I'd researched everything I could to figure out why others were concerned and the reason for my sheltered life but I couldn't find anything. My only hope for answers was in the archives which held the combined knowledge of our race.

"Are you ready?" Chantara asked, bouncing on her heels beside me.

"Yes," I faked an excited voice knowing she'd see right through it.

Chantara was the twelfth daughter of the Deva pack and the closest female to my age. We'd been drawn to each other but I found her power hungry motives annoying. Being the youngest and a female was aggravating since you had no choice or say in anything. Thinking of it made my blood boil but it was the society we lived in.

"The alpha-apparent of the Aibek pack is supposed to be here," Chantara whispered in my ear.

"Okayyyy," I sighed, not really caring about that pack's only alpha male.

"This could be my chance," she hissed, giving up her friendly tone.

"Better find him quickly," I whispered, rolling my eyes, already annoyed and ready to escape to a quiet place.

"There he is," a female voice whispered loudly and as one all our heads turned.

A breathtakingly handsome male leaned against a pillar, a glass in his hand absently swirling the liquid inside. His eyes were watching the glass but what drew our attention was the unbuttoned shirt revealing tattooed skin.

A thrill ran down my spine as I looked him over, my core tightening as a lock of light brown hair fell into his face. I could hear the increased heart rates of the women around me and smell the desire in the air.

Kuu, the alpha for the Aibek pack stepped to the gorgeous man's side and clapped him on the back while his beta tapped his glass to draw the room's attention.

"Normally the Gala is meant to showcase our daughters but this year I get to show off my son, Raff," the alpha announced, shaking his son's shoulder which caused him to look up revealing his seafoam green eyes to the room.

"Oh," I breathed, unable to stop myself.

He was gorgeous but his tattoos and hooded eyes made him seem sharper, more dangerous. It made my mouth water but I mentally shook my head. I had an objective tonight and swooning over some alpha-apparent wasn't going to distract me.

'He's a yummy distraction though,' *my wolf purred in my mind, basically drooling over him.*

I rolled my eyes in response. the sexual appetites of wolves were insatiable.

'You say that like you aren't one,' *my wolf chided, teasingly.*

The reminder of what I was and the lack of suitable men to satisfy my needs was jarring. Being sheltered had caused me to reach for fictional men that caused unrealistic expectations that no one could live up to.

The girls around me swarmed to the newly introduced alpha-apparent while I made my way to the buffet table. I filled a plate and grabbed a drink then made a show of walking around the room to "mingle".

Everyone's attention was on the group of women surrounding Raff so much so that no one paid me any kind of attention.

Which was exactly what I wanted.

I set my plate on the next table I walked by then asked those sitting to look after it while I went to the restroom. I mentioned to the waiter who I handed my glass to that I'd forgotten my lipstick in my coat and wondered where the coats were kept.

I made sure to tell at least three more random people that I was going somewhere to get something I'd forgotten or to see something or directions to meet someone in secret.

No one would know where I'd gone and if asked, be pointed in several different directions. It was perfect!

Now that everyone was suitably distracted I could get into the archive with plausible deniability.

I made my way up to the second floor cautiously. The Gala was a notorious time to sneak away with a lover. I didn't want to run into anyone and ruin my well-laid distractions.

Thankfully the second-floor corridor was empty. I listened and sniffed but didn't pick up anything that would indicate that someone had been up here.

The archive doors were at the end of the hallway and from my research it wasn't locked by anything special. I slipped off my heels, picked them up then sprinted down the hall. My bare feet made my passage nearly soundless.

At the door I withdrew two small tools that I'd hidden in my hair. Everyone turned a blind eye to the youngest female daughter which made it easy to learn certain skills. Like picking locks.

It only took me a few seconds to unlock the door, the satisfying click making me smile. I opened the door quickly and slipped inside, closing the door quietly behind me.

I pressed my ear to the door waiting to hear if I'd set off some internal alarm but after a few minutes of silence I knew I was safe.

Breathing out a relieved sigh, I turned to the room and smiled. Shelves and shelves of books filled the room while the smell of old books saturated the room. With a giddy smile I walked further into the room, my blue ball gown swishing around my bare feet.

I had all night here. No one would bother me and I'd finally get answers.

I didn't know where to start so I did what any bookworm would do and just chose a direction, a book shelf and a random book.

Flipping through it showed that it was a book about medicinal plants. Useful but not what I was looking for.

I moved on, searching for a section that was dedicated to prophecies, legends, or the Moon Spirit.

I'm not sure how long I wandered around the room before I stumbled upon a section of fairy tales. Feeling nostalgic, I looked through the tomes, enjoying the familiar stories I'd grown up reading.

Moonlight flashed across the spine of a book catching my eye. It was blue-grey in color and shimmered like an abalone seashell. I glanced up at the skylight seeing the moon shining down in all its beauty.

I took it as a sign so I slid the book from the shelf and turned around so I could set it on the long table that dominated the middle of the space. I flipped it open to the title page then frowned because I'd never heard of this collection before.

My fingers traced the words as I read them, wracking my brain for any mention of 'The Moon Spirit Origin and Philosophies'. A strange title for a book of children's stories.

I heard the door open then shut quickly behind me. I slammed the book shut and spun around excuses for being in here on the tip of my tongue but it wasn't who I was expecting.

Seafoam green looked at me, probably startled to find someone in here. I gulped thinking he'd sound the alarm or something, alpha-apparents were notorious for being tattletales.

His eyes flicked to the door then quickly turned the lock and I wanted to kick myself. Of all the rookie things to do I didn't lock the door once I'd gotten in.

Stupid. Stupid. Stupid.

Raff stepped away from the door just as the handle started jiggling like someone was trying to get in. We both froze, not even daring to breathe as we both watched the handle.

It stopped after a moment and I could hear faint footsteps leading away from the door. I couldn't relax, not when Raff was as tense as a deer facing headlights. His senses were probably better than mine so I remained still, ready.

Finally after a small eternity, Raff's shoulders relaxed and I could tell he was breathing easier now.

"Did you just escape your fan group?" I wondered, not bothering to hide my smirk.

"I'd been warned that they could be a bit..."

"Unrelenting?" I supplied but the word wouldn't do it justice. Alpha girls in the presence of an eligible wolf bachelor could be downright ruthless.

I noticed that his suit jacket was gone and his sleeves were rolled up his forearms and I figured out what had happened. He'd gotten hot and ditched his coat and rolled up his sleeves. He had to realize that he'd presented himself like showing steak to a starving dog.

Idiot.

"They just swarmed and I couldn't escape," he shook his head bewildered by the actions of horny determined alpha daughters.

"You're the only son and alpha-apparent. That combination would get any of them salivating for your dick," I didn't sugar-coat it. Poor dude was fucked.

"You're not swarming or salivating," he said, and I had to commend his deduction skills.

"Nope," I let the 'p' sound pop before crossing my arms over my chest.

The truth was, I was attracted to him but my expectations were so high that he'd no doubt fall flat.

'Pity,' my wolf sighed and I had to agree with her.

"Oh...you like your own team," he actually looked relieved and maybe a bit disappointed.

"No. I'm fond of dicks but haven't found one attached to someone who could use it," I shrugged, because the truth hurt even for me who didn't have one.

"You must have been disappointed by many dicks to be so jaded," he put his hands in his pockets, surprising me with his lack of defensiveness.

"I'm a virgin," I revealed looking around the room. Being a werewolf virgin was rare. Being sexually active was normal with werewolves. Wolves were pack animals and intimacy of any kind was needed.

"Really? Then how do you know..."

"That someone like you couldn't satisfy me? I've been sheltered my whole

34

life so I've had time to develop unrealistic expectations."

"But you don't know for sure," he countered, a teasing smile spreading across his face but I couldn't trust it.

"Are you volunteering?" I raised a brow at him, only partly joking.

"I'm not big on one-night stands," he said, and I was tempted to demand his bro card because he wasn't acting like a typical guy.

"Let me guess...you like long walks in the moonlight and cuddling," I laughed but then the look on his face made me stop.

"You have this preconceived notion about me and guys in general it seems."

"He walked closer, eyes fixed on mine, not in a challenging way but more curious."

"Men and dicks are a dime a dozen," I replied, standing my ground as he drew closer.

"I'm not like most and neither is my dick," he countered seriously like everything he said was fact.

"You're sure of yourself," I said, then gulped. He was closer now looking down at me while my head was tilted back so I could see his face.

"I have to be," he said, looking down into my eyes and I felt like for the first time someone was seeing me.

He didn't know who I was and I wasn't about to tell him. His nostrils flared and I could tell he could smell my arousal but that didn't mean anything. Attraction was normal, I reminded myself, smirking silently.

I took a breath and his arousal hit me like a punch to the gut. He was turned on by my rejections and I'd be lying if I said I wasn't intrigued by him.

"Sounds like a whole lot of lying," I commented, extra aware that his chest was nearly touching mine.

"Fake it until you make it," he said, leaning down until his hands were pressed on the table and his eyes were level with my own.

"I guess," I said eloquently, my eyes drawn down to his lips.

He leaned closer, green eyes boring into mine and this time they were full of challenge. A challenge that my wolf and I couldn't ignore.

35

I'm not sure who moved first but we were suddenly pressed against each other. We devoured the other with lips, teeth, and tongues.

His hands on my waist helped me sit on the table behind me. He pressed between my legs and I spread them letting him draw closer.

I ran my tongue along his bottom lip while my hands fisted and tore his shirt open. A sigh escaped when I ran my fingers over his chest, his warm skin and hard muscle underneath made me shiver with anticipation.

His fingers slipped through the straps of my gown pulling them off my shoulders. His hands were rough but they didn't hurt. They stimulated my skin making me want more.

His lips moved from my lips to my cheek, then my chin, and down my throat. I gasped when his tongue flicked out, tasting the skin of my shoulder and collarbone.

I pulled him closer, my hands gripping his shoulders so I could lean back, giving him better access to my chest.

"How do you get this off?" he growled, fingers searching my back.

"It's on the side," I lifted my arm so he could access the zipper.

"That's a weird place for it," he muttered, finding and pulling down the tiny zipper.

The bodice of my dress drooped and I didn't try to stop it but actually helped by withdrawing my arms from the straps.

Raff's hands cupped my breasts, thumbs flicking over my nipples. I moaned as my back arched, pushing my breasts forward. His lips were on my throat again kissing, caressing, tasting.

Heat gathered in my core, liquid fire dripping through me hot enough to burn. His touch was both cooling and scorching at the same time.

I needed more, needed him closer.

My hands found their way to his belt and I tugged on it impatiently.

His chest rumbled at my movements while his hands took over loosening his belt and unbuttoning his pants.

He paused, pulling back so he could see my face and I could see the question in his eyes.

"If you stop now I swear to the Moon Spirit..." he interrupted my threat with a kiss that curled my toes.

I began pulling my skirts up and he helped me then ripped my panties off in one movement that set me on fire anew.

"Fuck!" He growled, cupping me and finding me dripping wet.

I laid back while he pulled my hips to the edge of the table. He grabbed the material of my skirts and pulled my dress off, tossing it aside.

A moment of clarity struck me as I watched him look down at me completely naked. A blush heated my cheeks as moonlight danced over my skin making it nearly glow.

His eyes were aglow with desire as he looked me over. I wouldn't be surprised if he smirked then walked away, he'd proven he could get me naked. It would be the ultimate 'fuck you' but...he didn't. Instead he leaned down and ran his tongue through my slit.

My hips bucked and I cried out while his hands clamped onto my thighs, holding them down and open. He licked me then swirled his tongue around my clit before sucking. Fingers found their way inside me, curling forward. His mouth latched onto my clit, sucking and flicking it until I couldn't take it anymore.

My muscles clenched as an orgasm took me, my heels were on his shoulders and if he wasn't holding my thighs down I would have squeezed his head like a watermelon.

"Shit! Oh shit," I panted, my legs relaxing and I swallowed trying to make sense of what just happened.

Raff kissed the inside of my right thigh smirking as my leg quivered against his cheek.

"Now...imagine what my dick can do." His words made a shiver skate down my spine and my wolf purred in my chest.

"Mmmm," was my reply as he stood over me.

"Speechless?" He cooed, with a self-satisfied grin on his face.

Before I could figure out a reply he kissed me and I could taste myself on his lips. The head of his cock teased my entrance as his tongue dove into my mouth, his hands combing through my hair, spreading it out on the table.

"I want to taste you again," he growled, fingers tightening in my hair pulling, my head back.

I moaned, low in my throat as he ran his lips over my exposed throat, teeth scraping the sensitive skin.

"Please," I begged, my body on fire and the only thing that could douse it was him.

"Please what?" He grunted, moving his hips so his cock continued to tease me.

"Fuck me," I commanded, running my nails down his back then dug them into the muscles of his ass.

He pushed forward, sliding into me with ease before he stopped making me growl.

"Just hold on, little wolf," he grunted, torso quivering. "You need to adjust."

I took a moment to consider what he was saying then realized when he pushed a little further hitting resistance. The shock of pain was unexpected and I gripped Raff's shoulders.

"Shhh, it's okay," Raff spoke softly, running his fingertips over the skin of my face.

I nodded, then swallowed looking up into his eyes and feeling safe. This was a vulnerable time for any female and joking aside I was glad I was experiencing this with him.

"Thank you," I whispered, feeling suddenly emotional as tears pricked my eyes.

"Do you want to stop?" he asked, seriously.

I shook my head, taking a deep breath in through my nose and making a conscious effort to relax. I'd read books where the heroine lost her virginity so I knew that slow and relaxed was the way to go.

"Are you sure?" He asked so sincerely like he cared which was surprising.

Somehow this casual fuck had turned into something more serious.

"I'm sure," I answered, leaning up and pressing my lips to his. "Keep going."

He nodded, against my lips then moved to my neck, kissing and nipping while he slowly pushed into me.

The invasion wasn't unpleasant, just different than what I expected to feel. Raff's tenderness and thoughtfulness made what most would consider a unpleasant experience a dream.

Seated fully inside me still kissing my throat, my hair wrapped around his fingers was an exquisite moment I wouldn't soon forget.

"Raff?"

"Hmm," he responded, lips working their way back up to my lips.

"I'm okay," I told him, my legs quivering with anticipation.

He withdrew slightly then thrust back in, making me gasp as sensations rocked my body.

"Ohhhh, do that again," I requested, gripping his shoulders again as he moved in and out slowly.

"What's your name?" Raff whispered in my ear.

"Faelynn," I answered, realizing that I hadn't introduced myself before.

"Faelynn," he repeated, my name coming from his mouth sent a thrill through me.

I arched my back, moaning as his cock slid in and out of me in a slow methodical way. It was erotic but I needed something more, the slow movements weren't enough.

"More," I pleaded, looking up at the full moon as it shone down through the skylight.

Raff propped himself up on his elbows then quickened his pace making me cry out as he hit a spot deep inside. I wrapped my legs around his waist encouraging him deeper while it was everything I could do just to hang on.

My muscles began to tingle as he continued, I was yelling with each thrust on the precipice of an orgasm that would unmake me. Or rather remake me.

I threw my head back as my muscles clenched around his cock followed by waves and waves and ecstasy. White filled my vision and for a moment I felt like I was floating in a sea of moonlight.

Chapter Six

Faelynn

I ran my fingers over the intricate tattoos on his chest, remembering that night five years ago. I never thought that he'd found something he liked in me enough to warrant a second coupling. For months after I'd been on cloud nine but then when he was absent for the following Galas I'd figured he'd come to his senses afterwards about me.

"Heavy thoughts so early," Raff grumbled, his fingers tucking a strand of hair behind my ear.

"I just can't believe this is real. You're here...have been the whole time," I swallowed, feeling tears coat my throat. I should have searched for him or at least asked more questions.

"I was forbidden from contacting anyone and if anyone came looking they'd be exiled too," he replied, so quick to forgive and yet guilt weighed down my heart.

"For a time...I thought the worst of you." He'd been my first and to just disappear without a trace had been cruel.

"Do you still think that?" he wondered, his palm cupping my cheek in a tender caress that made my chest clench.

"No," I whispered, unsure how I had in the first place.

41

"It's all in the past. I'll be reinstated as my father's alpha-apparent today. It'll be like the last five years never happened," he said but I could tell even he had trouble believing his own words. "Once I'm reinstated I'll be going to your father."

"What?" I sat up alarmed. My father was the alpha for the Aruna pack which was known for being ruthless and violent. I'd seen it firsthand but the only saving grace was my father's commitment to tradition.

"We mated last night without permission or blessing from our families. I'll go to your father and ask for you."

"And if he says no?"

"He won't," Raff assured confidently, a dangerous glint entering his eyes that I'd never seen before.

"It's not just my father who you'll need to win over."

Raff nodded, his lips lifting into a smirk as he understood my meaning. Every pack had their alpha and the alpha-apparent. My brother Lorcan was stoic and as unmoving as a redwood tree. He'd followed in my father's footsteps, adhering to tradition while maintaining his cruelty. Lorcan had very little to do with me and I did my best to stay out of his way.

"It'll be fine," Raff assured me again but I wasn't convinced.

We'd been hasty last night, mating without regard for the consequences. Not that it mattered. I'd been going to the Gala for five years and no one had asked for my hand in that time. My father was no doubt tired of continuing to support me, his youngest and last daughter at home not yet bearing strong werewolf children.

My heart stuttered when I remembered what I had witnessed last night. What had caused me to run here in the first place.

Apollo.

Raff's palm on my cheek grew rigid and I realized I'd said the pack name out loud. His eyes were twin pools of green flames that flickered with barely contained rage.

"Apollo," he sneered, sitting up and pulling me until I was straddling his lap. "Why were they after you last night?"

I blinked, recalling how I'd overheard Candri and Chantara discussing for my mission to figure out what it meant.

"I...I overheard...Candri at the Gala last night," I began, drawing closer to Raff trying to absorb his strength through my skin. "I have a silver patch of fur on my thigh when I shift. They mentioned a ritual where they needed my blood and...Candri's seed."

The growl that vibrated in his chest was terrifying while his jaw was clenched so tightly I thought he might break a tooth.

"I intended to sneak into the archives to find out what I could about what they were talking about but I was caught, so I ran."

Raff had become stone; his muscles were tense while his eyes had taken on the glow of his wolf. He nearly vibrated with murderous rage and I wondered why I wasn't frightened then remembered we were mated.

"You have silver fur?" Raff asked, once he unclenched his jaw.

"My wolf is white but I have a small patch," I answered, looking down into his eyes letting him see the truth in mine. "I've heard whispers but have no idea what its significance is."

"I've heard stories..." Raff muttered, his eyes growing distant like he was trying to remember something. "I'm more concerned about this ritual."

I was too now that I'd been reminded of it. Raff's thumb freed my lip from my teeth, before he leaned forward and kissed me. His hands cupped my face while his lips seared mine. I opened for him and he swept his tongue in to battle with my own.

I groaned as heat filled my core, spreading through my whole body. My hands buried in his hair while my thighs spread further apart, allowing me closer to him.

His cock was hard between us and I gasped when his hands gripped

43

my hips pulling me closer. His head rubbed through my folds while he continued to devour my mouth.

"Faelynn." Raff groaned my name as his lips moved down to my throat.

My head fell back as his hands ran up my side then up to caress my breasts meeting his lips.

"Raff," I moaned his name while running my nails over his back.

A buzzing sound startled both of us, followed by a relentless pounding on the door. I could hear muffled voices but wasn't able to make out any words.

"Fuck!" Raff swore, picking me up and setting me behind him.

I grabbed the sheet and pulled it so it was covering my body, my eyes wide with alarm.

"Who is it?" I tried to ask as quietly as I could. If we could hear them they could undoubtedly hear us as well.

"Aibek wolves coming to collect me," Raff muttered, searching around then grabbing something from the floor.

"Why?" I wanted to reach for him because I was frightened but wasn't sure if I dared.

Raff turned around sharply, reaching for me and jerked me closer to him. He'd pulled a shirt on but hadn't found any pants so he was naked from the waist down.

"It's alright, love," he reassured, hand cupping the back of my head and holding me to him. "They're here to escort me to Aibek and my father."

"What should I do?" I asked him, feeling this overwhelming need to stay near him.

"I'll arrange transport for you to return to Aruna."

"No, Raff," I felt compelled to say, grabbing his shirt collar.

I couldn't stand the thought of being away from him, not when the bond was still so new between us. Newly mated couples were known to lock themselves away for weeks at a time with only each other for company.

"I know. The bond doesn't want us apart and neither do I," he gritted out as my fingers gripped him harder. "We have a chance of fixing things with our families but I have to be reinstated first."

I nodded against his chest, understanding what he was saying but hating it all the same. He needed to reestablish himself with his pack while I needed to calm my father and pray my absence wasn't noticed by too many.

"What about Apollo?" I wondered, the thought of Candri touching me made my skin crawl.

"I'll deal with them as soon as I'm reinstated," he promised, speaking in the dual tones of him and his wolf, making it impossible to lie.

"I'll find my own way home. It'll be better that way. Just...be quick about it," I ordered him as a smile spread across my face.

"I swear to you that I'll come for you as soon as I'm able," his words growled and I could hear them rumble from his chest.

I smiled, pushing away from him though it felt like my heart was ripping from my chest.

"Make it quick," I advised him, steeling myself for his departure.

He kissed me, hard. Slipping his tongue into my mouth, leaving behind the taste of him.

"I won't allow the sun to set with us apart," he said, then tore himself away, grabbing pants before leaving the room slamming the door behind him.

I covered my mouth to stop my scream of agony as his footsteps faded away.

Chapter Seven

Raff

Leaving Faelynn in my room all alone and newly mated was one of the hardest things I've ever had to do. Next to of course lying to her. If my wolf hadn't agreed with the action he would have stopped me. Wolves took the protection of their mates seriously even by their human half.

I opened the front door barely holding onto my control. The wolves on the other side dropped their gazes immediately, the small one in the back even whimpered.

They escorted me down the stairs but I use the term lightly. I had no desire to leave my mate in such a vulnerable state and the fact I needed to chafed me. I pounded down the stairs hard enough to stomp right through them.

My wolf tried to calm me but we were both low on fuses. The last thing I wanted to do was go see my father so he could reinstate me...not when Faelynn was in my bed.

Fuck!

The thought of her alone up there unprotected nearly had me foaming at the mouth. I took a deep breath, sucked up my anger and despair then shoved it to the side. I needed a clear head for this if my plan was to work.

After my sentencing, I was obsessed with Faelynn and wanted to know everything about her. I replayed our conversations and other things so many times over the years I could recite them from memory.

She told me she'd snuck into the archives to look up answers. I didn't pry then but I remembered the book she'd read in between our love making. For our first times we were ravenous for each other and I remember interrupting her reading several times.

The book was a collection of fables and philosophies but who could really tell the two apart. I read the story of the silver wolf who was destined to unite the packs under one rule and from the line produce the Alpha Seeker.

It was just a story, but looking back maybe I'd known on an unconscious level that she was this fabled wolf. For the past five years I've been studying and training, trying to become the strongest alpha so they'd never be able to keep me and Faelynn apart again.

I exited the bookstore, seeing the black vehicle waiting on the curb. I fought a sneer as a wolf opened the door for me, head down so his eyes were hidden. I could smell his submission but it did nothing to calm me. I needed my father's submission. Once I got that I could take my place as alpha of the Aibek pack and from there start to change this fucked up hierarchy.

The door shut and the sound grated on my nerves, setting my teeth on edge. The other wolves piled into the vehicle, eyes downcast with an air of fear.

I closed my eyes, breathing deeply through my nose, pushing the thought and scent of my mate to the back of my mind. I needed to concentrate on the coming task. My father needed to see a contrite son who was willing to conform before he'd reinstate me and I *needed* to be reinstated if Faelynn and I stood a chance.

"I'm glad you're back," a voice said, making my eyes flick open and narrow on the speaker.

"Why's that?" I asked, knowing full well that the state of my pack had deteriorated since my absence.

"Your father..."

Another wolf elbowed the speaker in the gut, cutting off his words.

I didn't need to hear what he had to say because I knew. My father's reign had gone downhill in the last five years. He had many children, all female. It took him years to conceive a son who was exiled the day after his first Gala. The shame had been written clearly on his face at my sentencing; neither had he spoken up on my behalf. He let me be exiled without speaking up for his only son.

He was a coward and a weak alpha. I wouldn't allow his weakness to continue. I'd strip it from him then use it to bring peace to my pack before going after my mate.

First I had to be calm and accept my father's reinstatement. Once I was alpha-apparent again I'd be able to tear control of the pack away. I'd be alpha by the end of day with Faelynn by my side.

I let the thought of the future consume me while my wolf secretly reminded me of the plan. Our plan had taken an unexpected turn but the rest of the plan was sound.

"Are you excited to be back?" The same young wolf asked before the other wolf elbowed him again.

"I am. It's been a long five years," I commented, eyeing the wolf who kept elbowing the younger one.

"We're glad your sentencing is over," the elbower said, though his words didn't match the distrust in his eyes.

Wolves needed a strong leader in order to thrive. The addition of the wolf soul to the human invited wildness and darkness that only the Moon Spirit or a mate could temper. Until a mate was found the Moon Spirit would offset the wilder instincts of the wolf through the alpha. That's why a strong alpha was needed to keep the darkness at bay while allowing the wolf to live and find his mate.

"As am I," I answered, feeling calmer than I had before. The distance between Faelynn and me was growing wider by the moment and I clung to her presence in my mind. The thought of her nearly white hair running through my fingers as her scent filled my nose was enough to make my cock twitch.

The gates that guarded pack Aibek opened as we approached and my stomach muscles tightened. Trees lined the driveway looking exactly how I remembered them. The manicured lawns spoke of the hard work my pack took at being presentable while underneath the facade was the rotten core.

A massive log cabin came into view, nestled between the trees like it had grown out of the ground. Log pillars were set in intervals acting like a more rustic cousin to a southern plantation manor. Huge windows dotted the front of the structure, bringing in natural light while giving the occupants a beautiful view of the area.

This was home. I missed and hated it equally.

The car pulled up next to the porch stairs and stopped. The rest of the wolves piled out and I followed them, straightening to my full height once outside.

"Raff! My son," my father called out, hurrying down the steps.

He was a good head shorter than me and while I'd been busy building muscle my father had been letting himself go. His stomach extended well over his pants while his belt looked strained. I fought a sneer when he clapped my shoulder and pulled me into a hug. He smelled of wine and sex which made my thoughts turn to Faelynn.

"Welcome home," he said, pushing back so he could see me.

I let a smile curl my lips though I was sure it didn't reach my eyes. He looked pleased to see me, which I supposed was good. I held nothing but contempt for the weak alpha but he was my father and I had to bide my time.

"Thank you," I said, feeling my wolf raise his hackles.

"We've got a feast waiting and a celebration planned for the following days. I've invited the other packs to attend." He nearly bounced with excitement.

"I don't feel like a feast or celebration, I just want to get back to my title," I replied, looking around at the gathered staff and onlookers.

"Yes! I'll reinstate you right now. Then we feast," my father spoke loudly then clapped. "My only son who was exiled for five years has returned home! I name him my alpha-apparent and successor!"

The crowd around us whooped, hollered, and clapped while my father beamed around at them all. I kept my gaze down to hide my face and tense jaw.

"Send a notice to the other packs that I have my successor back," my father ordered a staff member who nodded then trotted off. "Come, let's get you settled."

I followed as my father turned around and headed back up the porch steps. The doors opened wide at our approach, the colorful glass sending rainbows over the entryway walls and floor.

Walking down the hallways was surreal I could remember them but I couldn't recall any memories that didn't make my teeth clench.

My childhood was spent dodging abuse from my father and the staff. He'd ordered the staff to abuse me so I would become a strong alpha. I was forbidden to fight back since an alpha should never fight or subjugate the wolves in their pack. An alpha was to be of service and if that included a fist to the face or a kick to the stomach then I, as alpha-apparent, would take it all on.

I do not blame the staff. They were simply following the orders of their alpha. My grievance was with my father and his twisted upbringing.

As we wound our way through the maze of hallways, the walls felt like they were closing in around me which prompted my wolf to push forward. He forced my left hand to grip my right, the bite of pain reminding me of Faelynn and her mark on my flesh.

We could do this. We needed to do this.

The doors to my father's private study opened at our approach. The staff member he'd ordered earlier was standing beside the desk with a missive in his hand.

"They've all acknowledged," he said, handing the piece of paper to my father before bowing and going to stand in the corner.

"Sit, my son. Let us talk about what has happened these long five years apart."

I sat in the chair opposite my father's desk, the surface covered in stacks of paper that had a layer of dust. I fought the eye roll because my father was notorious for ignoring his duties. How he survived without me here to keep the pack running was beyond me.

"The pack has been thriving," my father lied, an easy smile curling his lips as he snapped his fingers. The man in the corner rushed forward with a bottle of wine then poured him a glass.

"Glad to hear," I replied, keeping my sarcasm tightly under control.

A wave of despair nearly overwhelmed me. My heart lurched in my chest as hopelessness followed closely behind the previous emotion. I would have stormed out of the room if my wolf hadn't stopped me and pointed out that it was Faelynn we were feeling.

Which just pissed me off more and the armrest on the chair creaked ominously. My wolf reminded me of the plan and told me that Faelynn wasn't in danger but feeling the effects of our mate bond. She was safe but missing us.

Fucking shit!

"The banquet hall is ready, Alpha," a voice announced from behind me, drawing my father's attention.

"Splendid," my father said jovially, pushing himself to his feet. "Come son, let's go celebrate with our pack."

I smiled then nodded, the vision of agreeability and a contrite son.

Hopefully I appeared happy to be back and like I'd learned my lesson.

My father led the way out of the room and down the hallway. The floorboards creaked under his feet causing my lips to pull down into a frown. The floor creaking wouldn't concern many but my father hated it. The fact that they did told me that my absence had been felt and not just by my father.

Looks like in small ways the Aibek pack had been showing their displeasure with the current alpha. It gave me hope that the pack would support me when I tore the position from my father.

Chapter Eight

Raff

The banquet hall was filled to bursting with wolves. More than I expected there to be. Somehow the pack had grown in my absence. I'd need to check on the welfare of each of my wolves in time. Hopefully with my mate by my side.

Quiet descended over the room as my father entered with me behind him. I could feel their eyes on me but I kept my eyes downcast. My dominance made wolves uncomfortable. The only one to meet my eyes and not cower was Faelynn.

"After a long exile, my son has returned after paying his penance to the United Packs. Raff has been reinstated and is recognized as my alpha-apparent by the other packs," he paused, looking around at the room. "My son has come home!"

Every wolf tilted their heads back and howled. The sound was a balm to my soul. I'd been alone for a very long time which would make a lesser wolf go mad. Exile was an extreme sentence for trespassing. Wolves were pack animals and if not part of a pack the animal would go feral.

My father stepped to the side allowing room for me to step forward and address the pack. I was expected to apologize for my actions and beg forgiveness for putting our pack in a vulnerable state.

I took a moment to gather my thoughts and think about what I wanted to say.

"My exile was…unexpected. It was lonely and at times maddening," I began speaking loudly so every wolf could hear my words. "I'm sure you all are expecting an apology and while I am sorry that I've had to spend the past five years away I am not sorry for my actions that led me to being exiled."

Silence answered my words and I glanced up to be sure that everyone was still in the room.

"Five years ago on Gala night I met an alpha's daughter in the archives. Our hiding place wasn't open to everyone but it was secluded. I fell in love with that woman and it took me extraordinary strength to keep my wolf from claiming her that night."

Gasps around the room followed my declaration as did whispering. I was admitting to almost losing control of my wolf in order to mate a complete stranger.

"To spare her punishment I admitted to the crime and I do not regret it. I'd do it again to keep her safe. I intend to make that woman my mate as she's the only one able to look me in the eye." I lifted my head so I could look around the room. "I have been reinstated as the alpha-apparent and I intend to rectify my actions."

Everyone in the room shuffled uncomfortably at my words. I gave them all a moment as I kept kept an eye on my father in the periphery.

I felt my wolf rise to the surface ready to lend me his strength. I gathered my own then reached for the power I kept securely locked away inside my mind.

An alpha's power and his inner strength that comes directly from the Moon Spirit until a mate is found then the strength is doubled by our connection. Our mating was still new, the bond not yet able to fully solidify. I wouldn't draw on her strength. I had plenty.

My power unfurled from the well deep inside, coaxed by my wolf. I let it fill me for a moment before I pushed out into the room.

Everyone present dropped to their knees, the pressure of my strength too much for them to shrug off. Whimpers filled the room but I ignored them and instead turned to face my father who was still standing but barely.

"What…are you doing?" He wheezed, cupping his glass while his other hand gripped his chest.

"I'm taking what is mine," I answered, pulling more power and letting my eyes meet his.

"Why?" He asked barely above a whisper as he sank to one knee before me.

"Because in order to claim my mate I need to have a pack and be alpha. That way no one will question my claim," I held his eyes, watching as his other knee dropped with the other.

"You can't…" he said, real anguish in his voice.

He knew what I was doing. Every alpha-apparent forced the pack away from their fathers. It's how it was done though many didn't wrest it away for a couple centuries at least. It took that long to gain enough strength to rival your sire.

I was a rare case. I'd had the power ever since I hit puberty. My wolf advised me to bide my time, then we were exiled which gave me ample opportunity to hone my power and strength.

I'd been content before to let my father continue to rule but when I found Faelynn I knew it was time to become the alpha she needed. When Faelynn told me about her silver spot I knew that the story I read in that book was true.

My mate and I's line would eventually produce the Alpha Seeker. I wouldn't allow an inferior alpha, like Candri, to claim Faelynn. She was mine. As was this pack.

I knew it. Could feel it in my very soul.

A presence I'd never felt before touched my mind and I started but my wolf calmed my racing heart.

'It's our mate reaching out to us,' he informed me. *'She's worried and only wishes to soothe.'*

The Spirit only knew what she was feeling coming through the bond from us.

'I've suppressed all but our determination. She doesn't know what we're doing but is supporting us all the same,' he said, my head filling with his admiration and love for our mate.

'We don't deserve her,' I told my wolf who agreed with me wholeheartedly.

Didn't mean we wouldn't do absolutely anything for both of them. Even become an alpha so I can claim her and keep her with no repercussions.

Anything for our mate.

During this whole conversation I stared at my father. I'd watched as his eyelid started twitching and could smell when he broke out in a sweat.

He finally dropped his eyes after ninety seconds which was longer than I thought he would last. I smirked then straightened so I could look around the room.

No eyes met mine and I could see that some of the more dominant wolves were shaking tried to break through my power. They couldn't. It was as absolute as my convictions.

I looked back at my father, seeing him for the cowardly man that he'd become. His power had diminished drastically when my mother died and again when I was exiled. It proved that my father was a weak wolf to begin with, how I became so powerful was a question only the Moon Spirit could answer.

"Take him away," I ordered my father's guards who were all kneeling. I lifted my power from them so they could stand.

"You ungrateful bastard," my father managed to seethe before my power silenced him.

'Take it,' I instructed my wolf who reached out and grabbed the pack bond.

He yanked and the connection broke away from my father. He groaned when it snapped, causing pain, something I hoped I'd never experience. My wolf growled in triumph as the pack bond attached itself to his mind.

My vision went white as the influx of thoughts from my pack streamed through our thoughts. My chest rumbled with a growl and I gritted my teeth, determined to ride out the alien feeling as we adjusted to being alpha.

Finally.

My vision returned slowly until I was blinking back tears as the overhead lights threatened to burn my retinas. I looked around and was pleased to see that everyone gathered were on their feet looking unsure but excited.

Glancing beside me I realized that my father was still on his knees. A snarl ripped from my throat as I turned my gaze to the wolves I'd ordered to take him away.

"Apologies, Alpha, we're not sure where you want us to take him and his scent is...different," one of the guards said, keeping his gaze on my feet.

"Take him somewhere he'll be comfortable. His scent is different because I changed it." I turned away hoping to stop any further questions about his scent.

"Yes, Alpha," the guard murmured followed by footsteps and dragging sounds.

"Alpha," a man's voice said, drawing my attention from the crowd. "I...was your father's beta."

I watched the poor man swallow before his eyes met mine and his jaw

57

flexed. I held his gaze for almost a minute before he was forced to look away.

I smirked, then extended my hand to him, "I'm happy for you to remain beta."

His shoulders relaxed before he reached forward with his hand, fingers wrapping around my forearm. He smiled as I shook his hand and I returned the gesture.

"What's your name?"

"Narvi, Alpha," he answered, stepping to my side so we could face the room.

"Please, eat," I spoke loudly to the room gesturing to the tables laden with food and drink.

A wave of surprise overcame me and I immediately recognized that it was coming from Faelynn. I wondered what she was surprised about when it changed suddenly to terror then quickly to disgust.

'Moon Spirit, take me,' a female voice whispered through my thoughts, making me jerk.

"Are you alright, Alpha?" Narvi asked, concerned in his voice.

'Faelynn? Can you hear me?' My wolf growled in my mind as the emotions from our mate continued growing more and more urgent.

'What's happening?' I asked my wolf who I could feel reaching out to our mate's wolf.

'I don't know,' he replied, frantically.

"Alpha?" A small tentative voice asked and it took an incredible effort not to rip into the poor wolf.

"Yes?" I queried, turning half my attention to the newcomer.

It was the servant from earlier who had waited on my father. He was short and mousy with a button nose and russet colored eyes.

"Th...the mating event after the Gala is scheduled for tonight," he gulped, speaking to his shoes and I thanked the Moon Spirit for wolf hearing.

"Am I required to attend?" I asked not in the least bit interested in going.

"Yes, Alpha. Th...there's to be an Alpha family mating," he explained, and I knew that all alphas are required to attend the mating of that sort.

"Very well," I sighed, turning my attention back to the room but my wolf nudged me insistently. I turned back to the servant before he could take more than a couple steps. "What packs are mating?"

"The Apollo alpha-apparent to the youngest of the Aruna pack alpha female," he said, then flinched as my wolf pushed forward ready to lose every bit of his shit.

Faelynn was ours!

Chapter Nine

F aelynn

I bit my tongue until I could taste blood as Raff left the apartment. I held my breath, listening to his footsteps fade, while fighting the anguish and panic.

Darkness shrouded my thoughts as I felt my mate traveling further and further away from me. My wolf was frantically trying to convince me to go after him.

'He's not supposed to leave us,' my wolf growled, rightfully upset.

Mating was different for every couple. The only similarities were the need for proximity and touch. If that meant sitting in a room and talking or fucking for days. The bond needed that time to solidify and all wolves respected that, but it was another matter for true mates. True mates were hardly ever found since arranged marriages were the norm.

Anger filled me at the thought of Raff not being here with me. I wasn't angry at him but at the circumstances that seemed to always keep us apart. I wanted to shake my fist at fate and curse him but I didn't want to anger him. Fate brought Raff and I together not once but twice. I prayed that we'd find our way back to each other.

My wolf growled unhappily but managed to get control of herself.

She didn't like this situation either but we had a task before us. Find our way home and prepare for Raff's return.

He would return.

I felt his conviction when he swore to come for me today. Raff was an alpha to be reckoned with, I could feel the dominance that ran through him. Plus he was mated now which granted the alpha power. We'd both been bred for this.

'We have to go home,' I told my wolf, taking my despair and shoving it way down.

'Yes we do,' my wolf reluctantly agreed.

I dragged myself out of bed, filling my lungs with Raff's scent and committing it to memory. I grabbed one of his tee shirts from the chest of drawers and a pair of boxers. No way was I going home in my ball gown. I already looked like I'd be doing the walk of shame.

I used the facilities then resigned myself to going home barefoot.

I wandered down to the bookstore and used the phone to call home for a ride. My directions were vague and I hoped I'd be spotted on the sidewalk instead of near here. Didn't want Raff getting into any more trouble.

I stuffed my dress into a plastic store bag then left through the door I'd ducked into last night. The bell jingled causing a small smile to lift my lips as I remembered the sound being a catalyst to change my life.

It was late morning but a brisk wind brought the scent of fall with it. I strolled down the sidewalk with confidence so no one would question why I was barefoot.

Three blocks later a black town car with tinted windows pulled to the curb. A young wolf hopped out and scurried to the sidewalk. He wore the light blue and teal colors of my pack and I recognized him as a member of the household staff. His eyes were downcast as he took the bag with my dress in it, then opened the door for me.

I ducked into the dark interior, breathing out a relieved sigh when there was no one in the backseat. Last thing I needed was my father or eldest brother coming to collect me. I hoped I'd timed it correctly so my return would go unnoticed.

The car pulled away from the curb and merged into traffic. Neither of us spoke as we drove through the city, returning to my pack's estate.

The Aruna pack's territory was located by a river surrounded by open fields then dense forests. It was a huge area to accommodate the large number of wolves in our pack. The estate itself looked like a plantation home. It was white with massive pillars at the front with ivy growing around and up them. If this place wasn't a source of despair I might find it charming, but charm couldn't hide the rotten core.

The car stopped in the circle driveway, the same young wolf jumped out to open my door. I stepped from the dark interior into bright afternoon sunlight. The sun on my skin felt incredible and I soaked in the feeling while subconsciously reaching to the newly formed bond with Raff.

I could feel his anger and impatience but had no idea why he was feeling those things. Nevertheless, I sent soothing thoughts through the bond, helped by my wolf.

"This way," the male wolf said, gesturing toward the enormous white door. "Your father has asked to see you."

"I need to change," I replied, ignoring his outstretched arm and instead turned toward the left side of the house.

"I'll inform him you'll meet with him promptly." The warning was clear but I brushed it off. My father had no reason to be upset with me, the Gala was the only excuse needed.

There was a side door hidden by ivy that seemed to only be used by the staff and me. It was tricky to find but if you knew it was there it was easy.

I opened the door, letting sunlight into the darker interior, glad to see that no one was waiting for me. Not that I expected it but you couldn't be too careful.

I closed the door already missing the sunshine and brightness. Hopelessness settled into my bones and I fought the panic and exhaustion that quickly followed. I hated this place. It was beautiful on the outside but on the inside, I was the only one who could feel the shadows lurking behind every corner.

Patting the door seemed stupid but it was my way of letting the outside know I'd return. The walls of this house were a cage and it was suffocating.

A deep steadying breath did nothing to calm my nerves, so I pulled up my big girl panties and made my way to my room.

"Lady Faelynn," my maid, Creola greeted me as I closed my bedroom door.

I nodded at her knowing from her polite words and tones that meant someone was watching and probably listening.

"I need to dress. My father is expecting me," I instructed her, watching as she moved to my closet which was filled with frilly, ruffled gowns.

My father picked my wardrobe only letting me pick my dress for the Gala each year. I'm not sure why he insisted on dressing me up like a doll but it was disgusting and I didn't have a choice. Either he or my brother made all decisions about me and I was more than ready to get out of here.

Creola held up a baby pink dress with white petticoats. I sneered at it with disgust but managed not to throw up as the stiff material settled over my body. I slipped my feet into soft pink ballet flats complete with bows.

I hate it here.

My wolf agreed then reminded me that this was the last time.

Creola brushed out my white blonde hair then curled strips to give my hair a beachy wave. My maid dressed me up like a doll and I hated it.

63

A knock on the door drew our attention as the male wolf who'd opened my car door earlier entered the room. His eyes were no longer down but looking up and I noticed that his eyes were a chocolate brown, observant, and familiar.

"Your father is impatient," the wolf said and my heart lurched. My father's impatience was legendary, not to mention, explosive.

"Alright, let's go," I said, waiting for him to lead the way out of the room.

The wolf smiled but it did the opposite of putting me at ease and instead had dread dropping into my stomach like a stone.

I followed him out of the room and down the hall. I sniffed the air cautiously but couldn't detect an unfamiliar scent which didn't bode well. This wolf had to be new but he also didn't smell like pack which was suspicious.

"Is Lorcan with my father?" I asked, doing my best to keep my words light and not full of fear.

"He wasn't there when I left," he answered.

I breathed out a sigh of relief. My father was a bastard to deal with but my brother would just make things worse. They were both sticklers for tradition but their resolve was ironclad. I didn't know what Raff's plan was but it had to be legit, completely by the book.

The door to my father's office was unassuming but just the sight of it had my stomach in knots. My escort opened the door and stepped aside so I could enter first then pulled the door closed once he was inside.

My father was sitting behind his desk in a massive chair that was designed to make him look imposing. His eyes, the same color as my own, flicked up when the door clicked shut.

"Father," I greeted respectfully, making sure to keep my gaze on his neck so I wouldn't upset his wolf.

"A moment," my father said, so I remained where I stood waiting for him to invite me closer. "Did you have fun last night?"

"Yes, I did," I responded softly, knowing that a soft submissive voice would go a long way to cooling his anger.

"Didn't see you much," my father intoned, making my heart skip a beat. "You were out all night."

It wasn't a question but I nodded my head hoping that he'd drop this line of questioning before I gave something away.

"Yes."

"Normally, I'd be upset but the one you were out with has come forward asking for your hand. Under the circumstances I'm inclined to agree." He put his pen down then looked me in the eye while steepling his hands in front of him.

I felt my heart leap. Raff was reinstated already and had come for me sooner than I was expecting.

"You'll be mated tonight for the Gala after party. I expect you to be in attendance, ready and willing." His voice was firm meaning he would not tolerate any arguments.

"Yes, Alpha," I replied, doing my best to hide an excited smile.

"Good, now go prepare. I took the liberty of ordering a dress befitting someone in my family."

"Thank you, Father," I bent forward in a grateful bow.

I turned to leave but there was a knock on the door. I stepped back allowing my escort to open the door.

His scent hit me first and my stomach curdled instantly. Candri stood in the doorway, his evil shrewd eyes were hooded and made shivers run down my spine.

What was he doing here?

My wolf growled in my mind and it was all I could do not to fidget as Candri stepped into the office. He cast his eyes over me and I saw the tick in his jaw and the twitch in his pants.

"Candri," my father called, standing and walking around his desk to shake the creep's hand. "I wasn't expecting you so soon."

"Thought I'd get a jump start on things," he smirked at me before turning to my father and shaking his hand.

"Anxious to become family?" My father chuckled while I felt like I was going to throw up.

"Family?" I asked before I could stop myself.

The venomous look my father shot me was a warning to keep my mouth shut.

"Of course," Candri said, reaching me and pulling me close. "Your father has agreed. We'll be mated tonight."

My wolf howled in my head as despair and horror filled my chest, choking me of breath. I reached for Raff, needing him but another emotion stopped me.

Shame.

Chapter Ten

R aff

'*Why can't you reach her?*' I growled at my wolf while I paced my father's office ignoring the mess of papers and broken furniture.

'*The bond is still new, it hasn't had time to mature,*' he replied, just as anxious and furious as I was.

'*Keep trying,*' I ordered, then turned my attention back to the room I'd just destroyed.

I needed to regain control before I did something stupid. The other alphas would support a mating between two packs so I needed to have ironclad proof that we were mated. The only way to prove that was to stand together in the moonlight, but I couldn't wait that long.

I promised Faelynn that I would come before the sunset but I needed the moon to prove my claim. The matings after the Gala were always held at sunset so I needed a plan to delay the ceremony.

I closed my eyes and took a deep breath trying to force myself to calm down so I could think of a plan.

'*Anything?*' I asked my wolf but he just shook his head.

I needed to get her a message somehow. She needed to stall for as long as she could. At least until the moon appeared so I could prove my claim.

"Narvi?" I barked, starting to pace the room again.

"Alpha," Narvi greeted as he entered the room.

"Does paranoid ex-alpha still have contacts in the other packs?"

"A few but they've died out due to lack of leadership."

"Tell me there's still someone in the Aruna pack." Narvi flinched at my tone before a thoughtful look covered his face.

"I think so. I'm not sure. We haven't made contact in months."

"Try now. I need to get a message to the young Aruna alpha female." I gestured to the phone that was still intact after I'd destroyed everything.

"Alright," he said, moving to the phone and picking up the receiver. "What's the message?"

"Tell her to stall for as long as she can and that I'm coming for her." I growled the last part, but my beta didn't even flinch, which was a point for him.

He got busy with the phone while I got back to calming my wolf and myself down.

There is another option,' my wolf pointed out and I knew what direction he was heading.

It's not time,' I hissed at him knowing he had a point.

If we can't get her the message then what?' He asked, making me clench my fists and stopped myself before I tore into the walls.

It's our last resort,' I told him, wanting to keep an ace up my sleeve.

The truth was the packs were still living in the past. Things had changed and instead of embracing it the alphas clung to tradition and outdated thinking. The world was changing around us and it was time for the different packs to as well.

Younger generations like mine were tired of the hierarchy and bigotry. It was time for a new order and I'd spent the last five years putting it into effect. Plenty of wolves in every pack were ready to live as equals instead of the alphas ruling supreme. It was time to leave tradition behind us and work toward a united future.

I'd done my research and the appearance of the silver touched wolf meant change was coming. Faelynn's father had hidden her away, forcing her to live in solitude instead of embracing the gift that she was. Through her, things would have to change, the Moon Spirit demanded it. We could either support her change or fight it. I knew which side I was on.

"Message sent. My contact said that he'd pass the message to the youngest alpha female's maid," Narvi announced, slamming the phone down.

I ran my hands through my hair while sending up a silent prayer that everything wouldn't go to shit.

* * *

Faelynn

I was in shock and was led back to my room by the male wolf whom I now realized came from the Apollo pack. Candri must have sent out cars with my description. Thankfully the car had brought me straight home.

My thoughts were all over the place as was the bond. I couldn't make out anything from Raff except for his steady presence in my mind which did little to comfort me.

What do I do now?

I was straight up fucked. There was nothing I could do, no way to fight this ruling. My father had absolute control over my future, I had no say in any of it.

Rage boiled just below the surface while frustration at my lack of choice made me want to pull my hair out.

Instead, I tore the doll dress from my body, tearing it into pieces. That wasn't enough so I lunged for my closet and threw the doors open, my hands grabbing at the pastel colors.

"Faelynn?" Creola asked, speaking quietly as I continued to rip my wardrobe apart.

"I refuse to mate that bastard!" I screamed, throwing shoes across the room. "I'm trapped here."

"Is there anyone you can reach out to? Lorcan?" She asked, her voice becoming frantic.

"He'll not go against my father," I screeched, ripping my hair down.

"Someone else? Someone on the outside we could get a message to?"

I shook my head, I knew of one person but I have no idea if or what he could do anything. We were mated but it could be ruled unfit and my mating to Candri would replace it.

The thought of having Raff ripped from me was enough to stoke my rage into fury. This couldn't happen, not when I finally found him again. He was mine and I was his. I wouldn't allow anything to keep us apart.

"Creola, go to the kitchens and get me provisions," I ordered, standing and digging through my chest of drawers until I found jeans and a dark tee shirt.

"What do you plan to do?" she asked, worriedly.

"I'm leaving."

"You can't! You know what happens to wolves with no pack."

I did know what happened to packless wolves but that was a path I'd rather choose than mating someone who doesn't love me. Candri only wanted me for what I potentially was. I was tired of males ruling my life. This was the last straw.

"I know Creola, but it's a fate I'd choose for myself rather than the alternative."

She nodded, her lips pressing into a thin line as determination hardened her features. "I'll do what I can," she said before rushing from the room.

I grabbed a black drawstring bag and began filling it with essentials including my human ID. I was facing a life as an outcast and for the first time it didn't fill me with absolute fear.

"Faelynn," Creola said as she entered the room, a brown satchel over her shoulder. "I've got a message for you."

She handed me a slip of paper that looked like it had been torn from an envelope.

"A wolf I've seen before but never spoken to discreetly slipped it in my pocket and whispered it was for you."

I hesitated. I trusted Creola but unfamiliar wolves seemed to be everywhere and couldn't be trusted.

I unfolded the paper and quickly read the words scrawled on it.

Faelynn

Stall for as long as you can. I'm coming for you.

-Raff

My heart lurched in my chest while I reached for the bond, reached for him. I felt a flicker of awareness then cursed knowing that the bond hadn't had time to mature yet. The words renewed my hope and my determination. If I left, Raff would find me wherever I'd go and that would be the best way to stall.

"I have to leave," I told Creola who nodded her head.

"There's guards posted at every entrance but if we can get you to the stables, you could escape then."

"Right. I don't suppose we have forged notes anymore?"

"We have one that could work," Creola ran to my bed then ran her hand under the mattress. "Here it is."

She pulled a slip of paper out then smoothed it on the covers. I looked over her shoulder and read it quickly, a grim smile spreading across my lips. It could work.

"I'll accompany you. We'll say you need to work off some of your nervous energy."

"We'll need to be quick," I warned, handing her my bag and slipping a riding dress over my clothes.

We left the room, shutting the door quickly behind us. There was a buzz in the air and I knew it was from my impending mating. A celebration would be held and every member was invited. We hadn't had cause to celebrate in a long time. I couldn't blame them for being excited.

We made our way down the stairs, our stride sure and determined. Creola handed the guard the note while I stood there impatiently staring at the guard, ready to challenge his wolf if I needed to.

The wolf guard nodded then stepped to the side and opened the door for us. We hurried through it knowing that time was not on our side.

We quickly walked to the stables that were located behind a grassy hill. It was a simple structure shaped like a barn with stalls with plenty of room for the horses. It was a pastime of my father to breed horses and I had to give it to him because he was a master of very little, but he excelled at this.

We entered the stable and I ducked into a stall while Creola went to have my horse saddled for me. I heard a nicker from behind me and turned to find a colt and his mother. Her ears were tilted back slightly in warning as she blocked her baby from me.

I hushed her and spoke softly to her and after a moment she relaxed.

These horses had been raised alongside us wolves and learned overtime to trust our wolf scents. She was a beautiful roan and even though she'd been raised around wolves instincts could not be silenced.

"I won't hurt you or your baby," I whispered to her, being sure to keep my distance so I didn't spook her further.

"Faelynn?" Creola called quietly.

"Creola, I'm here."

"Your horse is ready in the third stall," she instructed, then ducked outside to lead others astray.

I watched her go, wishing I had time to properly thank her for everything she'd done for me, to tell her I appreciated her.

I prayed she knew it.

I slipped out of the stall and hurried to the third one. My horse, Darling, was saddled and pacing, eager to get going.

I grabbed her reins then expertly swung myself up into the saddle. Usually I'd mount outside but I needed speed. Settled, I nudged her forward and she surged through the stall door then down the aisle to the back door.

The late afternoon sunlight shone brightly and I could almost taste my freedom, when something hard hit my head. I fell, landing on my side while Darling neighed above me.

I pushed to my knees, my head still ringing from whatever had hit me. I shook my head trying to clear the ringing when a booted foot kicked me in the side, knocking the wind from my lungs.

Wheezing, I rolled onto my back, my ribs screaming in pain as my accelerated wolf healing started to kick in.

My vision was blurry but I could see someone leaning over me. I squinted and the face cleared revealing Chantara's features.

"Hello Faelynn," she sneered before kicking me in the side again. "Leaving so soon?"

Chapter Eleven

F aelynn

Chantara dragged me back to the manor house by my hair. She continued to kick me in the torso so I couldn't fully catch my breath, while my wolf was too busy healing us so we couldn't shift.

The guards looked the other way as I was forcibly dragged through my home and up the stairs. I struggled against her hold and got a fist to the face for my troubles.

We need to shift! I snarled at my wolf whose attention was split between healing us and trying to force a shift.

My skin tingled then grew tighter, the shift was so close I could feel my wolf's fur on my arms.

"No shifting," Chantara ordered, then held a small black cylindrical device in front of my face. I lurched backward but her hold on my head was firm. She pressed the button and I closed my eyes a second before the pepper spray hit them and my nose.

My face burned like molten metal had just been poured over my skin. I screamed reaching for my face trying to wipe off the liquid but all it did was spread it over my face.

"A gift, my love," Chantara announced, flinging me onto the stone floor.

I rolled over and tried to open my eyes. I needed to see what was coming so I could fight.

"Bind her," Candri's voice ordered.

Hands pushed me over then wrenched my arms behind my back. I screamed again when the sore flesh of my face hit the cool stone and it seemed to burn even worse.

"She was trying to run," Chantara said, her voice taking on a seductive tone.

"Was she now?"

Footsteps drew closer to me but I was busy trying not to drown in my own fluids.

Hands wrenched me to my knees and I moaned as the burning slowly began to fade.

"Why were you running, Faelynn?" Candri asked, grabbing a fist full of my hair, pulling my head back.

I tried to open my eyes but everything was fuzzy and it made me sick to my stomach. I heaved hoping that would encourage him to get away from me. It had the opposite effect and I heard the air whistling before a hand slapped me across the face. My teeth cut into my cheek causing blood to fill my mouth.

I leaned over and spat out the mouthful of blood and saliva. I whimpered when I felt a presence drawing closer to me again.

"Ready to answer? Why were you running?" Candri's hand wrapped around my throat then he shook me like a rag doll when I didn't immediately answer.

He pushed me away in disgust. I landed on my back with my hands still bound behind me. A foot kicked me in the stomach and I wheezed out a scream as another hit my chest.

"Could it be that you don't want me?" he growled, wrapping his hand around my throat and picking me up. "The Alpha Seeker will come from my line."

I managed to muster up enough saliva so I could spit in his face. He gritted his teeth and raised his fist to strike me again.

"Stop!" Chantara said, grabbing his arm before he could land his blow. "She's baiting you."

Candri flung me across the room, my back hit the wall and I heard the bones in my hands and arms fracture. I slumped to the floor doing my best to keep my weight off my arms and hands.

"Don't you see," I heard Chantara say to Candri, "the line would end with her. Killing her will not get you what you want."

Candri growled audibly which meant that his wolf was beside himself. I'd challenged him by spitting in his face but he needed me alive at least until he got his heir.

I shuddered, just the thought of bearing Candri anything was enough to make me gag.

"Get her ready. It's almost time," Candri snarled. I heard footsteps then felt rough hands grabbing my shoulders and wrenching me to my feet. "I won't have my future bride spoiled."

I almost snorted, unbeknownst to him I was already spoiled. My father promised a virgin no doubt but I hadn't been one in five years.

Cantara kissed him then walked to the door, winking at him before she closed it. I watched the alpha-apparent warily but he didn't look in my direction. Just stood there, seething.

Thirty seconds passed then the door opened again. Creola and two other female staff stepped into the room followed by Chantara who held an unassuming canvas bag.

The two new wolves held a garment bag that could only be my mating dress.

"Get her dressed. Don't be late," Chantara ordered, holding the door open for Candri to exit.

The door clicked, then Creola and the others rushed to me, dumping the garment bag on the floor.

"Faelynn," Creola whispered, tears in her eyes. "I'm so sorry."

"This isn't your doing," I grunted as the bones in my arms started to shift.

"What can we do?" One of the other wolves asked, looking at me with anger and pity.

"Get me ready but take as long as you dare," I ordered them silently praying that Raff had a plan.

"How are we supposed to dress you with your hands bound?" Creola growled, ripping the shreds of material from my body.

"There's silver in the metal," I told them or I would have broken free of them already.

They all nodded before helping me to the bathroom so they could wash my hair and body.

"Don't worry miss, we'll make you look so beautiful he'll regret laying a finger on you."

The statement was meant to reassure but it just pissed me off. A mate should never lay a harmful hand on their mate and if they ever did their life would be forfeit.

My wolf shifted uncomfortably in my mind; her morose mood one only I guess at.. The bond had shrunk until all I could feel was a faint pulsing. I couldn't reach out to him or draw strength from his wolf and it broke my heart. I hoped that Raff was spared from feeling what had just been done to me.

The light from the sun dimmed as the three female wolves continued to get me ready for the mating I didn't want. I was trapped now wholly and completely. There was nowhere for me to run, no allies who would help me.

Despair filled me as my hair was curled and my fingernails painted. This all seemed pointless since I'd rather die than be Candri's mate. I held my hope for Raff close but if he couldn't come for me then I needed another plan.

The answer revealed itself when I was finally ready to get dressed. Chantara entered the room with Candri behind her followed by my eldest brother, Lorcan.

I stood in the middle of the room naked. My hair fell in delicate waves down my back while my skin had been scrubbed and moisturized until it nearly glowed.

I could feel all of their eyes assessing my nakedness but I wasn't self-conscious of my body.

"Beautiful, sister," Lorcan said, and I jerked my head up to see if he'd really spoken.

Lorcan's blue eyes were as hard as ice but I could see a flicker of something in their depths. Before I could puzzle it out, he blinked and it was gone though his jaw was clenched like he was biting his tongue.

I'd seen Lorcan around the manor but it had been years since he spoke to me. Creola mentioned that he was as cruel as ever but I always wondered if it was the truth or just rumors. I'm not sure which would be better.

"We need her hands unbound to dress her," Creola spoke, her eyes fixated on her feet.

"Of course," Lorcan said, withdrawing a metal key from his pants pocket. He moved forward then around until he was behind me.

I stood still as he used the key to loosen the small chain. My arms dropped to my sides, the manacles still fastened around my wrists needing a different key to unlock.

Creola and the other two female wolves quickly went to work binding me into the white dress. It was silky but it felt abrasive and tight on my skin. It was like a cage, trapping me in place. I tilted my chin up, refusing to let anyone see me upset. I wasn't male or the firstborn but I came from a strong line of alphas who would be appalled at this treatment.

Once dressed, Lorcan grabbed my hands and refastened the chain between them. Chantara approached me as my brother returned to Candri's side.

She set the canvas bag on a side table, letting the sides fall until a glint of metal could be seen. My heart sped up in my chest as she removed the metallic device from the bag.

It was a mating collar, made to subdue and force a female wolf to mate. Thick metal wrapped around my throat while two chains on the back of it were fastened to the cuffs on my wrists, when pulled down the chains would force my head back. Two sharp claw-like pieces were placed under my chin. If I tried to lower my head the chin pieces would cut me.

There would be absolutely no doubt that I was being forced into this mating.

* * *

Raff

The bond was no bigger than a pinhead which had me and my wolf raging. We could not feel anything from the bond now which made my anxiety spike. I just hoped that Faelynn got my message and was doing her best to stall.

I regretted asking her to stall. I could only imagine what she was going through with Candri's manipulations. If something happened to her I'd never forgive myself.

My wolf agreed with my sentiment though he was busy dealing with the wolf side of pack affairs. I was trying to do the same but my mate consumed my thoughts.

"Sir?" Narvi asked, jolting me out of my head and into the present. "Are you sure we should be doing this?"

"Doing what?" I flipped my pen around my finger, completely forgetting what we were doing.

"These issues can wait," Narvi said, flopping the stack of papers down on the desk.

"I can't concentrate," I leaned my head into my palms wanting to rip my hair out.

"Okay..." my beta retorted with a touch of exasperation. "We should talk."

"Where to start?" I grumbled, instinctively reaching for the bond.

"I know you were exiled but not entirely sure why?"

So I told him everything. Including the super secret traitorous things I'd been organizing behind the pack's back.

"The corruption is deep and widespread," I concluded, averting my eyes from his shocked face.

"So you planned all this because Faelynn's line will eventually produce the Alpha Seeker?" Narvi asked for what I hoped was clarity.

"Yes but Faelynn is my mate. I knew when I first saw her standing in a pool of moonlight. I'm not perfect by any means but I can't allow things to continue the way they have been. I'm not the only one who feels this way."

"No I don't suppose you are," my beta conceded, running a hand through his hair.

"I'll admit that the timing isn't ideal..."

"No it's not," Narvi agreed with a nod then sighed and sat back in his chair. "I rarely agreed with your father but I'm happy that you as alpha will bring change."

"Thanks," I said, fighting a smile as I subconsciously reached for the bond.

A knock on the door followed by a wolf guard poking his head into the room. "Your car is ready, Sir."

"Thank you," I said then turned to my beta who looked worried but ready. "We'll need to mobilize at a moment's notice."

"I wish we had more time to plan," my beta grumbled, climbing to his feet.

I mentally agreed with him but didn't say anything. No matter which way I looked at it, mine and Faelynn's future would be decided tonight. I just hoped we'd chosen the right path.

Chapter Twelve

Faelynn

"Don't fuck this up?" Chantara sneered, holding a blade to Creola's throat.

Creola would have me sacrifice her but that wasn't the kind of wolf I was. Instead I glared at my ex-friend wishing I wasn't locked in this contraption so I could spit in her face. I clenched my teeth and tried to keep my murderous thoughts out of my eyes.

'Her time will come,' my wolf assured me and I prayed it was soon.

"Go," Chantara ordered, jutting her chin at the door.

The Apollo guard from earlier held the door open then grabbed my biceps. My skin crawled at his touch and Raff's bite mark flared suddenly with heat. The guard sucked in a sudden breath and I wondered if he'd felt it too.

He kept his eyes averted but his grip on my arm loosened. If Chantara wasn't following with Creola still in her grasp I'd think about running but I couldn't.

Please stop this, I pleaded with the Moon Spirit. If anyone could stop this it was her.

I reached for the bond again fruitlessly hoping that it was open again. As much as I hated playing the damsel, I couldn't save myself without injury or murder. I'd just have to bide my time and hope an opening presented itself.

The guard guided me down the stairs and through the first floor. The halls were lined with our pack members wishing me farewell. Usually this was a time for celebration but being restrained and escorted by my soon-to-be-mate's guard meant that I wasn't doing this willingly.

I held my head high, extra aware of the sharp points that were resting under my chin. As unjust as this was I wouldn't cower; I was an alpha female with centuries of dominance running through my veins.

The front doors opened revealing a pearly white limousine complete with a chauffeur in a matching suit standing by the open back door.

With the Apollo guards assistance I climbed into the back and settled uncomfortably on the seat. I had to sit ramrod straight or risk puncturing my throat.

The guard slid in beside me and I did my best to ignore him which wasn't hard when I noticed that my brother was sitting opposite me. He wore a cream colored suit with an Aruna blue tie. His nearly white hair was pulled back into a bun at the base of his neck. He looked every bit the Ice Alpha that other packs called him.

The vehicle pulled away from the house and I was almost glad to be leaving this place behind. I didn't have any fond memories here. I hoped it rotted to the core.

The ride through the city was quiet and if I wasn't so uncomfortable I'd try to take a restful nap. My body had healed on the outside but lingering injuries and the mating collar kept me erect in my seat while exhaustion weighed on me.

The Apollo guard kept shooting sideways glances at me and I did my best to ignore him. I didn't need his pity nor did I blame him for following orders. He didn't have a choice just like I didn't in this situation which made my blood boil with rage.

"Are you ready for this, sister?" Lorcan asked, jolting me from my dark thoughts.

"Do I have a choice?" I shot the question at him wishing for a moment it was my fist.

"There's always a choice," he said, leaning forward in his seat.

"This isn't what I want but what other choice do I have besides suicide?" It was hopeless. I was restrained and locked in a contraption that forced my submission.

Lorcan opened his mouth to answer but the car jerked to a stop. The Apollo guard opened the door then grabbed my arm pulling me out.

The community building that hosted the Gala stood straight and tall, casting an intimidating shadow over me.

'We've come full circle,' my wolf whispered ominously.

Seeing this building again made my skin crawl and dread churn my stomach. Instinctively I reached for the bond and found it nearly gone. My heart clenched as pain and despair flooded my system.

I checked the sky and found that the sun was beginning its descent below the horizon. Soon the moon would rise and I'd be forced to mate, to carry Candri's mark for the rest of my life.

The prospect had tears forming in my eyes. This wasn't the life I wanted. I'd barely begun to picture a life with Raff and now it was being torn away from me.

"Let's go," the Apollo guard said, pulling me up the stairs to the entrance.

My wolf howled in my head and I fought the urge to join in her sorrowful song.

The main room was filled with chairs in neat rows with an aisle down the middle. Presumably where the bride would be escorted down to her groom. A very human tradition that we'd adopted, but instead of the happy couple vowing to love and respect each other for the rest of their lives I'd be forced to mate.

With this contraption on I'd be lucky if Candri demanded privacy, but knowing him he'd fuck me in front of a room full of people. That way no one could challenge Candri for the mating.

The thought of Candri's bite mark on my flesh made me want to run the other way. I couldn't, with the guard currently attached to my arm and the sharp points resting delicately near my throat.

I was trapped and that thought made my wolf feral.

'Keep it together,' I advised her, feeling my skin ripple as I suppressed the shift my wolf desperately needed.

The guard led me to a small room, depositing me in a chair while he guarded the door. I sat rigidly so the metal at my chin wouldn't cut me.

My wolf growled in a defiant way and a trickle of fire raced down my spine giving me surprising strength and resolve. I felt my fangs lower over my lips while fur sprouted from my skin.

"Whoa," the guard exclaimed, moving towards me away from the door.

I snarled at his approach which made him stop dead in his tracks. The color bled from his face as my nails grew into claws. This was the most I could shift without causing harm to myself which I didn't care about anymore.

I jerked my head to the side, feeling the sharp metal slice through my skin. Blood dripped from the wound onto the pure white dress. I repeated the motion until a steady stream of blood coated my neck and stained the front of the dress.

"What're you doing?" the guard hissed, looking appalled at my appearance.

"I'm showing everyone that I'd rather die than mate with that sadistic prime-alpha," I replied with a growl, letting my fangs bite into my lips.

He looked taken aback by my words then uncertain. He glanced over his shoulder at the door before returning his gaze back to me, a frown on his face.

"You can't stop this," he said resignedly which was exactly how I felt moments ago.

"I'm way past caring," I told him seriously as thoughts of Raff overtook my mind.

I recalled the way his hair felt running through my fingers. How his scent lingered on my skin and his touch seared my flesh.

Heat grew in my abdomen while moisture collected between my legs. The guard's eyes widened as my arousal filled the air in the room. He took a step back swallowing and trying to avert his eyes away from my heaving chest.

A knock on the door drew our attention before Lorcan opened the door. The muscles in his face tightened as he took in the blood staining my dress and my half-shifted form.

"She did it to herself," the guard said defensively.

Lorcan's eyes cut to him and the guard flinched like he'd been sliced with a blade. He stepped further into the room, eyes returning to my nearly feral state.

"You are unhappy," he commented, his white eyebrows bunching together like he couldn't understand why.

My chest rumbled as he continued to stare at me. It was strange to have my brother looking at me like he understood my pain.

The blood on my neck started to dry causing my skin to itch so I jerked my head, reopening the wound under my chin.

Lorcan drew closer, his hand wrapping around my biceps. His mouth opened like he wanted to say something before our father's voice reached us from the hallway.

"I'll bring her father," Lorcan spoke firmly.

Our father snorted before acquiescing without fighting further. Thankfully Lorcan was blocking me from view, not that I cared. I was beyond caring.

"Let's go," Lorcan said but his tone was different, empathetic maybe. He tugged on my arm before I could tell him that I didn't need his pity.

We exited the room together, Lorcan angling his body so he blocked me from sight.

My chest vibrated with anger but he just squeezed my biceps. I couldn't tell if it was reassurance or something else, not that it mattered.

I was led down the hall back toward the main room. The murmur of voices clued me in that the room was packed. Matings after the Gala were just as popular as the Gala itself.

My steps faltered a bit as I thought of all the people in the room watching as I was forced to mate. It was enough to give anyone pause.

"Keep going, Faelynn. Head up, shoulders back, you're an alpha's daughter and you have a right to show your displeasure." Lorcan spoke softly to me, while his words brought steel back to my spine.

My wolf surged forward, ready to do whatever it took. She was determined to make this mating one to remember.

Saliva began to pool in my mouth and coat my fangs. I straightened my shoulders and raised my chin. Lorcan was right, I was an alpha's daughter and I'd be damned if I didn't fight this every step of the way. Raff would and I knew he'd expect the same from me as his mate.

Lorcan turned the corner and the murmuring in the room turned silent as every head turned to see the blushing bride. Instead they saw a nearly feral wolf who was dressed in white that was soaked red.

A snarl ripped from my throat as the points pricked me causing more blood to drip. Lorcan pulled me forward and my wolf snapped at him and the people sitting by the aisle. Everyone pulled back, scared to be too near the mad she-wolf who obviously didn't want to be here.

Candri stood at the end of the aisle looking handsome though his face was red with fury or embarrassment, maybe both. He walked down the aisle toward us, the muscles in his jaw flexing as he tried to remain composed.

A snarling bark left me as Candri tried to take Lorcan's position. I didn't care for either one of them but I'd take my chances with my brother if I had a choice.

Saliva dripped from my fangs as Lorcan handed me over to my future mate. My wolf snapped at him, unable to control herself as she longed to rip his throat out.

Faster than I could react, Candri backhanded me. My head jerked to the side as the points cut into me causing fresh blood to pour down my throat.

I heard a growl nearby but I was so dizzy from the hit that I couldn't pinpoint who it came from.

Candri pulled me forward but I fought him as best I could with my hands tied behind my back. After a minute of tug of war, Candri gave up. He grabbed a fist full of my hair and dragged me the rest of the way to the front.

My wolf whined and yipped the whole way, putting on a show for everyone gathered. A mate was supposed to be precious, a gift from the Moon Spirit. Our society had abandoned the belief and made matings a political process.

Candri threw me on the floor away from him. I glanced at his face and found that his wolf was staring out at me so I bared my teeth at him and stared into his eyes defiantly. I was challenging his wolf. I was just as dominant as he was, maybe more.

Unbidden my eyes drifted to my father who watched everything with an exasperated look on his face like he couldn't wait to be rid of me. I'd grown beyond needing my father's approval years ago but it still stung. Lorcan beside him looked angry, his jaw was clenched and his nostrils flared. I could almost see the inner battle for him but I wasn't sure exactly what it was.

A growl brought my attention back to Candri who was seething at me while Chantara sat in the front row behind him, a sadistic grin on her face. They were definitely a pair and deserved each other.

"Get on with it," the alpha from the Apollo pack, Mawu, ordered.

Candri pounced like he had been waiting for the verbal order from the beginning and I wondered if Mawu was in on the scheme too. Would make sense actually. This whole arrangement would need the approval of both alphas and I couldn't imagine Mawu not using his influence to get what he wants.

Candri grabbed me and hauled me to my feet, his grip hard enough to cause bruises. He grabbed a fist full of my hair and yanked my head back exposing my neck. I growled and thrashed trying to break his hold but he had the advantage. I gathered saliva and managed to spit at his face. His chest rumbled at my defiant behavior before his claws sank into my scalp. I hissed as the sting registered, I bit my tongue so I wouldn't whine and tasted blood.

The roof and wall behind us was open to the sky and I watched as the full moon began to rise over the horizon as the last rays of sunlight disappeared. Teeth scraped over my exposed throat making me tense. This was it.

"What the…" Candri muttered.

I swallowed with difficulty but couldn't see what had caused Candri to pause, yet I was eternally grateful for it.

A crashing sound came from the back of the room drawing everyone's attention. Candri's hand loosened and I was able to tilt my head to see what the ruckus was all about.

Raff stood in the doorway, prone forms littered the hallway floor as wolves surged into the room. Blazing green eyes looked out of a face that was twisted with rage. His nostrils flared as he breathed in the room no doubt getting a good whiff of my blood.

"Drop. My. Mate." Raff commanded, his words were spoken in the dual tones of him and his wolf as power radiated off him in waves.

Candri fought the command but I could feel his muscles loosening unconsciously.

"Put her down!" Raff snarled, stepping further into the room a glow

89

beginning to shine from his arm.

My bite mark.

His mark on my neck was undoubtedly glowing in response to his. Moonlight cascaded down so the Moon Spirit could bless our mating by making it known to all.

"Too late," Candri sneered, pulling me closer and forcing my head back again. "We've made a deal. She's mine."

Raff roared, the sound loud enough to rattle the windows and shake the floor. A wave of power rolled out over the room causing everyone to fall to their knees including Candri. I tried to roll away but his grip on me was hard and unyielding. Candri wasn't about to give up without a fight.

"She's no one else's. She's mine. Drop her now," Raff demanded but I couldn't see him though I desperately wanted to. His mark on my neck began to tingle and burn, reminding me of our promise to each other. He was right.

I didn't belong to anyone else.

Chapter Thirteen

Raff

A red haze descended over my sight like the world had suddenly been bathed in blood. The alpha-apparent at the front of the room still held Faelynn against him. She was covered in blood while the glint of metal reflected the moonlight. The mating collar was an abomination that shouldn't exist. Fury rose inside me when I saw the contraption trapping my mate against her will.

'He's mine,' my wolf growled in my thoughts.

'Get in line,' I retorted, not at all amused by him.

"I challenge you right here, right now," I said, not bothering to loosen my hold.

I could feel the other alphas straining against me but it was no use. No one had the strength or determination. I'd spent the last five years gaining strength and plotting how I'd overturn this world. It was time. *Now or never.*

I removed my power from everyone and smirked as they all took a collective breath. All the alphas rose to their feet, their wolves daring me to look them in the eye. I didn't bother with their challenges. I was alpha now which meant an even playing field but that wasn't entirely right. They were all old, out of shape, and possibly senile.

"Fine," Candri spat, finally dropping Faelynn who slumped to the ground, making my heart clench.

'She's exhausted,' my wolf reassured us both as Candri made his way down the aisle unbuttoning his shirt and cuffs.

Wouldn't want to ruin his mating clothes.

That thought had my wolf pushing forward until he was looking out at the pompous wolf who refused to make eye contact. His form began to change, fur sprouted from his skin while his ears morphed into wolf ears.

These types of challenges aren't just about fighting. They were designed to test both parties in alpha power, dominance, and control. Good thing me and my wolf wanted the same thing.

Candri stopped five feet from me, his nearly shifted form a good indication of his control. He was taller now, covered in grey fur with canine fangs filling his mouth. His nose was elongated enough to be a short snout and his eyes were glowing with power and dominance.

The weaker wolves in the room fell to their knees at Candri's display of power. I scoffed, wondering why he accepted my challenge when I'd proven moments before I was much stronger than any alpha in this room. No matter. I'd play this game then rip his throat out and deliver it to my mate as a gift.

A sinister smile crossed my lips as I let my wolf come forward. Tingles descended over my body starting from my head. I shivered as the change morphed my body into something that was between man and beast.

I rose another foot in height and black fur erupted from every inch of skin. My face shifted almost completely into a wolf while my tail sprouted from the base of my spine. My knees twisted backwards as claws grew from my fingers and toes.

Candri's eyes grew wide at my transformation while gasps could be heard from the surrounding witnesses. I was a fully shifted wolf but still retained my human physique while the other wolf couldn't even manage a tail.

Pathetic.

My jowls lifted in a snarl and the next second I was hit with a wave of power that was immense. Candri had thrown in the strength and might of his pack behind him. It was significant, I'd give him that but it was only a drop in comparison to mine.

I stepped forward, shrugging off his power like a horse would a gnat. My hand wrapped around his throat and the next second I was roaring only inches from his face.

I'll never forget the look on his face or the terror in his eyes. He was a big fish but he'd just met a bigger one.

"Yield, little alpha?" I asked him gutturally, my mouth not meant for speaking.

I felt rather than saw his head move back and forth in a no gesture. I grinned toothily before I opened my jaws as wide as they could go, knowing it was big enough to swallow his whole head.

"Wait!" a voice cried from the gathered crowd.

My jaws snapped shut and I turned to see Mawu, Candri's father, making his way through the crowd toward where I held his son.

"Come to bargain, Alpha?" I commented, the words were garbled but understandable.

"Yes," the man said, looking concerned and fearful for his son's predicament.

"No," Candri managed to wheeze out.

"She's obviously his mate. Is she worth dying over?" Mawu asked and my chest rumbled at his insinuation.

Faelynn was definitely worth dying over. I'd die for her in a heartbeat but the alpha wolf's word gave me pause. Seems that Candri hadn't told his father why he wanted to mate with the Aruna pack's last alpha female.

"Keeping secrets from your alpha?" I mused, finally locking eyes with

Candri who immediately dropped his gaze, submitting to my wolf.

"What secrets?" Mawu demanded but I wasn't about to tell him who exactly Faelynn was or what her line would produce. If it became common knowledge then her life would forever be in danger.

"She's the silver wolf," a female voice interjected from the front of the room. Everyone turned to see an average looking wolf holding a knife to Faelynn's throat. My heart leapt when I saw blood trickling from the sharp points and knife.

"Silver wolf?" Mawu asked, confused.

My muscles coiled ready to tear her throat out in order to silence her but before I could Faelynn's father stood up and faced the Apollo alpha.

"My daughter has a silver patch on her all-white wolf," Faelynn's father announced to the room, making me growl angrily. "It's been rumored that her line will produce the Alpha-Seeker."

"It will come from Apollo's line," Candri growled, summoning some spunk.

"She's mine," I snarled into his face, ready to end his life right here right now.

"Hold on...she could produce the Alpha-Seeker?" Mawu asked Faelynn's father with a jealous gleam in his eye.

"Raff?" Faelynn's voice reached my ears and my eyes flicked to where she was. "Yours. Always."

Those words made my chest swell. It was time and my wolf agreed with me, so I did what I needed to do to save and protect my mate.

I reached out and grabbed the connection that every alpha had to their pack and yanked it. I pulled it all away from them and my wolf took over that connection just like we'd done with my father.

Pain exploded in my head but my wolf quickly took over blocking the pain as he took on every single wolf in every pack. I could feel my body growing as power coursed through my body from the different packs. I could hear their voices as they felt the connection to their alpha severed.

I gritted my teeth, determined to take this all on. This was what the Moon Spirit needed me to do in order to protect my mate. I couldn't allow her to live in a society that would force matings for political gain.

Awareness around me returned slowly as my wolf began organizing the different packs in my head. We wouldn't be able to control all of it for long but hopefully long enough to change things. Nearly every wolf in the room had collapsed to the floor except for those that had already pledged themselves to me. I made eye contact with every alpha-apparent in the room and each nodded agreement with my actions.

"What happened?" Faelynn's father asked from the floor, staring at me and then his son in turn. His eyes had sunken into his skull while his skin was an ashy color.

"I've taken control of the packs," I answered, meeting Lorcan's eyes for a moment before he crouched down so he was on more of a level with his father.

"What have you done?" he asked his son whose face held no emotion.

"It's time for change," Lorcan replied, tilting his head to the side. "Change would never happen with you in charge. It was time anyway."

Lorcan stood and turned his back on his father and former alpha.

Every other alpha-apparent was having the same sort of conversation with their fathers except for Candri who was slumped on the floor, unconscious. He had never been a part of this, too caught up in the power and prestige that came with the title. I used my foot to turn him over wondering what should be done about his corrupt pack. I didn't trust him and I certainly wouldn't be handing him the Apollo pack, not after everything they'd done to me and Faelynn.

Faelynn.

I jerked upright, my eyes finding Faelynn immediately. The female had dropped to the floor unconscious, freeing my mate from her clutches. The blood-stained front of Faelynn's mating dress made my wolf frantic. I rushed to her, cupping her cheeks with my hands. Her bright blue eyes were looking at me with wonder, love, and devotion. It made me want to beat my chest like a caveman.

"How do I get this off of you?" I asked her, wanting to rip it off but knowing it would hurt her if I did.

"There's a key," Lorcan called to me then pointed at the female behind Faelynn.

I grabbed the wolf, unconcerned that she flopped around like a rag doll. I reached for the power of her pack then sent a command for her to wake up. Her eyes popped open and all the color drained from her face as she looked me in the eye.

"Release her," I ordered, using every bit of dominance and power I could muster before releasing her.

She reached into her pocket and withdrew a key. She scooted closer to Faelynn and released her hands though there was another lock to remove the contraption. I growled when she fumbled with the key and tried it in the other lock.

"I...I...I need the other key."

"Who has it?" I demanded, ready to reach through and force this person to come free my mate.

"Raff! Behind you!" Faelynn yelled, her blue eyes wide with terror.

I spun on my heels, managing to duck the blade that was aimed toward my neck. Without thinking I punched my fist forward into Candri's chest expecting it to knock him back but instead I broke through into his chest cavity. Before I could react, my hand wrapped around the still beating organ in his chest and pulled it out.

Candri slumped to the floor, his father shouting in anguish but the sound had turned to a buzzing in my head as I held the wolf's heart in my hand. I hadn't meant to kill him but my wolf pointed out that we couldn't trust him and that he deserved death after what he did to our mate.

I squeezed the warm organ in my hand before turning to Faelynn who was staring at me with wide eyes. There was no fear in them, only concern and gratitude. I walked toward her then carefully deposited the bloody mass on the floor in front of her. She gulped but didn't hesitate to say thank you, which was an acceptance of my actions.

"He has the key," Faelynn whispered, her eyes lifting to meet mine.

I searched Candri's body and found the key in his pants pocket. I tossed it to the female wolf and commanded her to once again release my mate. It seemed to take her forever to fit the key into the slot and unlock it but I knew it was only a few seconds.

Once free Faelynn launched herself at me and I caught her. For the first time since we parted I could feel the bond again, our connection. I felt her so deep inside me that I couldn't tell what was her and what was me. The scent of her blood made my mouth water and my wolf urged me to claim her again and rid her of everyone else's scent but mine. Instead, I squeezed her tightly to my chest ignoring my bloody hands as the world righted itself.

"Raff?" a voice asked, and I growled at the interruption.

"They need you Raff," Faelynn whispered, pulling back so she could look up at me.

"I need you," I retorted more harshly than I intended.

"I'm not going anywhere." She smiled up at me and I felt a tension I'd been carrying ease at her words.

This was the beginning of a new regime, we were at the forefront of it, but Moon Spirit willing we'd bring about much needed change. If Faelynn's line would one day produce the Alpha Seeker, then so be it. We'd give our people the best chance of withstanding the tribulations to come.

Moon Kissed

the first book in the Alpha Seeker Series is now available for preorder!

Preorder Moon Kissed Here

Keep scrolling for a sneak peak at the first two chapters!

Chapter One

P^{earl}

Some might say I had a death wish since I walked alone through the forest to my house every night. They would be right, but they didn't understand that it was a balm to my soul. The solitary stroll calmed my wolf and me as we made our way to our childhood home that had, sadly, seen better days.

It was home though, and that was what I couldn't give up.

'Or won't,' my wolf grumped, pushing against me until I felt like I'd bust out of my skin.

'Calm down! We'll run when we get home.'

She settled a bit, but I could feel her annoyance.

The truth was, the packs ran nightly, but I never joined them. Being ostracized made one leery, but they also kept detailed records of each wolf and its markings. My wolf was all white, and while that wasn't unusual, it wasn't common either.

White wolves had a certain stigma about them. I didn't want to draw attention to myself, and the best way to do that was not to run with the others. There was another reason, but I wouldn't allow myself to think of him. The bastard who betrayed my family to our pack's alpha to better his own standing. He'd been my best friend, and now just the thought of him made me sick.

My wolf whimpered in my head, not daring to contradict me.

I'd cut him out of my life, and I'd be damned if I ever spoke to that son of a bitch again.

My wolf retreated, knowing I wouldn't be good company with him on my mind.

I let the silent walk do what it had always done and soothed my boiling temper. The moon was high in the sky already, the leaves of the trees casting shadows on the forest floor. I breathed in the scents—leaves and wet dirt, with just a hint of the rain that fell early in the day.

Delicious.

A tingle ran down my spine when my dilapidated home came into view. It had seen better days, but I did what I could to make it livable. It was covered in ivy, like the trees were determined to reclaim it. The windows were dark, but that didn't bother me. If the lights were on, then I'd be concerned.

Do no harm but take no shit.

That was a phrase I grew up hearing from my father. You think the thirty-year-old washed-up quarterback was a sad story? It has nothing on my father. He used to be in the upper echelon of the packs. An enforcer.

A century and a half ago, an incredibly strong alpha male changed things. He took the bond away from the alphas of that time and gifted them to the wolves he deemed worthy. He dispersed those who actively worked against him, letting them be absorbed into others. He didn't stop there though. He tasked those wolves with acting as pack enforcers. Basically, spies. They remained secret for security reasons.

It was a good idea in theory, but corruption runs deep.

The Daywa pack's enforcers were stripped of their duty and basically cut out of the pack. I was seven when my father lost his station. My family watched as he wasted away, sitting in his easy chair, drowning his wolf in alcohol and drugs.

I was eleven when he died, sending my mother into a spiral that ended with her taking her own life. Regardless of my father's actions, he was her mate, and being without him was torture she wasn't strong enough to handle.

Over the years, my siblings grew up and moved away. Most found mates or love, one even found a human to shack up with, but I didn't.

The only thing I'd managed to find was a love for reading and a few close friends. They didn't know of my history and never would if I could help it.

I rounded the house, preferring to enter the dwelling through the back door. I set my bag by it then went about stripping my body naked. A shiver moved through me, not from the cool temperature of the season but from pure excitement.

My wolf surged forward again, filling me up until I knew that this time I'd probably burst. The change came, splitting my skin open so my muscles and bones could rearrange themselves into another form. White fur erupted all over my body, causing me to shake off the temporary itchy feeling.

We bounded off the porch, my wolf ecstatic to be free of the confining human skin. I chuckled, receding so she could do what she wanted. I could relate to the trapped feeling. Being alone had felt like a sort of prison that I couldn't escape. The Moon Spirit only knew how frustrating it was to hold everyone at a distance, always watching my back.

A howl from the pack's run echoed through the landscape, causing my wolf to freeze and tilt her head. I mentally shook my head at her; we couldn't go with the others, not yet. She whined in reply but reluctantly agreed with me. It wasn't time.

A breeze picked up, ruffling our fur and bringing with it an unfamiliar scent. Another wolf had been close. We trotted off into the woods surrounding the house, nose to the ground, following the unfamiliar scent.

'*Female*,' my wolf growled, annoyed that another would dare come onto her territory.

'*Someone passing through?*' I didn't want to get into a territorial fight tonight.

My wolf ignored me and kept tracking the scent until we reached the small pond that no one went to but me, it seemed. It was secluded and didn't have enough water to swim in. Light from the moon lit up the pond, making it glow against the gloomy surroundings.

Our chest rumbled with contentment. Regardless of the past or the future, this was home.

A snap to our left drew our attention. Our ears stood erect as we listened to the sounds around us, waiting for more clues.

The underbrush around the pond grew quiet, and I could hear the blood pumping through our body. A steady rhythm that reminded us of the moonlight that gave our species life.

A howl rang out somewhere in the distance while a wolf-like sneeze sounded from behind us.

We whipped around, our eyes searching through the trees for any sign of another wolf. We growled, a low menacing sound, warning whomever it was that we weren't to be messed with.

Dried leaves crunched under paws as the other creature stalked closer. Our jowls lifted, and our head lowered, ready to tear this whomever it was a new asshole.

As if reading my thoughts, a yip followed by a soft whine reached our ears. We huffed through our nose, listening as they retreated the way they came.

Satisfied, we turned back to the pond then settled down on our haunches.

"Well, that was rude," a voice said, interrupting the pleasant silence.

We jumped to our feet, turning so we could face the newcomer. A woman stood by the bank dressed in a white shift that seemed to reflect the moonlight.

"Oh, cut it out," the woman grunted, walking to a log and sitting down on the rough, weathered wood.

Her bare feet dug into the soft dirt, like she's never felt the mud between her toes. That thought gave us pause. We took a closer look at the woman and found that her shift was tattered and dirty. She looked like she'd just escaped from somewhere.

"Stop that growling and come here," she said, grumbling about wolves who didn't listen.

My wolf approached hesitantly, wondering if we should call for help. The woman's face had been hidden in shadow, but as we drew closer, they shifted.

She was old. Wrinkles lined her face, but they couldn't hide the hideous scars that ran across her cheeks. Claw marks.

The sight of it made us freeze. We inhaled, catching her scent as we did. She was a wolf; it was *her* scent we'd followed out here in the first place.

We surged forward, and my wolf let me take the lead. The change was quick, and then I was back in my naked human form.

I knelt in front of her, not shy about my bareness. Wolves were pack animals, and that extended to us shifters. She looked like she'd been starved of contact for years, decades even.

Her fingers were twisted and mangled, like they'd been broken repeatedly so her wolf healing couldn't keep up.

Anger gripped my chest, and my wolf snapped her jaws in my head.

"Who did this?" I asked her softly.

"Never mind." She waved away my concern, and I noticed more scars on her wrists. She'd been restrained.

"Where'd you come from?" Maybe I could backtrack and find the ones who did this and make them pay.

A hand slapped my cheek, bringing me out of my rage-filled daze.

"Didn't you hear me? Never mind about me. It's too late anyway." She muttered the last part then readjusted her seat on the log.

"My house isn't far from here," I offered, thinking she'd be much more comfortable in a chair.

"There's not much time," she said then coughed into her hand. It sounded wet, and her lungs rattled. I could hear the sickness in her chest.

"Okay." I drew closer, hoping she'd give me more details.

"These packs aren't what they used to be; there's a darkness running through the minds of the dominant. Thoughts of greed and cruelty."

I felt her words in my bones. I had experience with wolves who were selfish and didn't care about who they stepped on to get to where they were.

I nodded, understanding what she was saying while her eyes grew unfocused, like she was remembering a painful time.

"I was the last hope to find an alpha that would unite the packs and do away with the corrupt hierarchy, but I was imprisoned instead." Her lips trembled, and tears spilled from her piercing ice-blue eyes.

"Why?" I knew that the alphas were only out for themselves, but I hadn't thought they'd go as far as imprisoning female wolves. What did she mean by alpha to unite the packs?

"I'm the Alpha Seeker," she whispered, her hand squeezed mine as she looked me in the eyes. "My mate was supposed to be the one to unite the packs and finally bring peace. I never found my mate, and now it's too late. I'm dying and need to carry out my duty to the Moon Spirit."

I opened my mouth to ask what she meant when her hand clenched. I tried to jerk away, but she was too strong.

The blue in her eyes disappeared and was replaced with silvery-white irises. Her other hand grabbed my elbow as a bright light flashed. Fiery pain raced up my arm to my shoulder then my neck. I froze, unable to scream or even move as the pain reached the base of my skull. White filled my vision, and I feared I'd pass out from the agony.

Suddenly, it stopped, and I found myself kneeling before the old woman. Her appearance had changed; no longer was her hair silvery-white but gray and lifeless. Her icy blue eyes were now dull and flat.

"What did you do?" I whispered, her hands sliding off my arm, like she no longer had the strength.

"You're the Seeker now," she said then coughed. The gurgling sound in her throat reminded me of drowning. "Find your mate. He'll unite the packs."

"I don't understand."

She laughed weakly, swaying on the log, so I reached forward and gripping her shoulders to keep her from falling to the ground.

"My failure is now your mission. Be careful who you trust but know the Moon Spirit will guide you." She swayed again, the gurgling sound from earlier growing louder.

She slumped on the log, and I heard the moment her heart gave out. I helped her limp body to the ground, sweeping her gray hair away from her face. She looked at peace, and I was glad that she was no longer in pain.

A rustling from the other side of the pond drew my wolf's attention. I squeezed the woman's shoulder one more time before standing and slipping into the trees just as several dark-colored wolves bounded into the clearing. Saliva dripped from their mouths, and I could smell their anger.

I stopped and ducked behind a tree, heart pounding as I listened to see if they would come after me.

"Dead," a deep voice spat in disgust.

"What now?" another voice asked.

"Be vigilant. Another Seeker will be born. I want to know the second that she's found," the deep voice growled, and recognition hit me like a shot to the heart.

Rylan.

Chapter Two

Rylan

So much for thinking time would ease her hatred.

'*I told you it wouldn't work,*' my wolf growled at me, furious.

I didn't blame him; I was pissed at myself too for insisting that we leave. I thought it would be good for us and for Pearl.

'*Don't blame her,*' my wolf snarled, angry at me—for good reason.

Wolves saw the world in black and white while humans could see every shade in between. I thought we needed time apart. After everything between our families, I thought space would heal what had been done.

We'd known from a very young age that Pearl was our mate. Our friendship was rock solid. I'd have done anything for her, and I knew she would have done the same for me.

But when it comes down to family or friendship... I regretted choosing the former.

'*If we'd stayed, she would have forgiven us eventually.*'

I couldn't exactly disagree. It was his argument from the start.

My wolf shook out his black fur before picking up the pace, sock feet eating up the ground as we ran to rejoin the pack.

Checking on Pearl was the first thing we did when we returned, and

I wasn't about to stop. My time away, touring and learning from the other packs, taught me that being away from her was a special kind of torture. It did the opposite of soothing my soul and instead put it through a woodchipper.

'*Trust the Moon Spirit; she knows best,*' my wolf reminded me, and I wanted to rip my ears off.

He was right though. I had to trust, to hope, that things would work out.

'*Nephew, we are returning,*' my uncle, the alpha, said through the pack link.

I sent him my acknowledgement back but kept our thoughts separate from the rest. It was our first night back with the pack, and my new station hadn't been announced yet, so I could enjoy the anonymity for now.

'*She's hurting,*' my wolf decided to point out, and a pang of guilt hit me in the chest.

I vowed to him and to me that we would fix this. Whatever it took, whatever she needed, we'd do it.

'*What about the pack?*'

It was a good question; one I'd have to do some soul searching to answer.

The pack house came into view when we crested a small knoll. It was nestled at the base of a grassy hill, surrounded by thick forests. This was a dream for pack land but so were the other packs' lands so while it was ideal it wasn't special.

A cloud shifted, bathing the valley in moonlight. A shiver ran down our spine as the light touched us, like the hand of the Moon Spirit herself was stroking our fur.

'*We'll make this right,*' I promised the twinkling light of the stars.

'*Rylan? Get your ass down here,*' my cousin Ledger ordered through the pack bond.

My wolf's jowls rose at the order. Ledger was the alpha's son, so he technically *could* give orders, but it rubbed my wolf the wrong way.

My thoughts went to the journal I was given from the Aibek pack when I left. It the alpha mated to the original Alpha Seeker that he'd written while in exile. I've read it three times and felt like the words were written for me to read.

The well of power that he had deep inside explains the swirling heat I felt but couldn't access. The journal showed his journey of finding and harnessing it so he could be the alpha the packs needed for change.

Too bad it didn't work.

Something was blocking me from accessing this well of power, and I had a pretty good idea what it was.

Pearl.

The journal's wolf had found his mate before he was exiled, and while I knew that Pearl was mine, I just couldn't get past the guilt to confront her.

'*Rylan*,' Ledger barked in my head, sending a bit of power to jolt me. It didn't, but I wasn't about to tell him that.

'*Coming*,' I replied quickly, giving my wolf the reins and letting him track where our cousin was.

We ran back into the woods, smelling the same scents we did as children. This was home, but oddly enough, it didn't feel like it anymore.

My wolf slowed, which turned my attention back to what we were doing. As we drew closer I recognized that this place was close to Pearl's childhood home.

My heart lurched in my chest as anger bubbled up at the thought of Ledger being anywhere near her. As far as evil goes, my cousin had a generous helping built up by my uncle.

The hidden pond by Pearl's home was one that was as familiar to me as if it were my own childhood home. Days spent with Pearl by the water, soaking during the hot afternoons, then curling up in the shade, praying for a breeze—those were the happy days before shit went to hell.

We pushed through the branches, a growl ready in our throat, only to discover Ledger with three other alpha-apparents standing around a body.

My wolf tapped out and gave me control again. The change came over me quickly with only the briefest twinge of pain.

"What happened?" I asked once I was back on two legs.

"She escaped," Ledger said flatly, like finding an old woman's body in the woods was a normal, everyday thing.

"Escaped from where?" I bent down, ignoring my nakedness to get a better look at the woman.

"The cage," Dane, the alpha-apparent from the Aruna pack, answered.

"An old wolf in the cage?" I murmured, not expecting an answer since the cage was meant for the most ruthless of criminals and rogues.

"She was, perhaps, the most dangerous one in there," Alder said, solemnly looking at the prone form on the ground.

"Dangerous?" I snorted. She was an old wolf who'd lived out her life in the cage, just long enough to escape it.

Why? I almost asked out loud but bit my tongue when Ledger snarled and then kicked the body.

"She was the last Alpha Seeker," he growled, wide chest heaving as he reigned in his anger.

"Alpha Seeker?" It was a term I was familiar with but only from the journal, the author very careful to protect his mate's identity.

"The Alpha Seeker is a legend that no one's heard of recently because she's been in the cage for nearly a century," Dane commented, acting aloof but I could tell he was bothered by the discovery.

"I'm not familiar," I lied, crouching down to get a better look at the old woman's face.

"She or her line seeks out the one true alpha, the one who can unite the packs."

Unite the packs?

Now there's a thought, one I was also familiar with since the journal came from the Aibek clan.

"She's dead now though," Alder pointed out the obvious, making me fight an eye roll.

"It doesn't matter," Ledger grumbled, still angry, but it had turned to exasperation. "The Seeker power is passed down to the next generation."

"Do you know if she had children? A mate?" There had to be an explanation of why she felt it so important to escape when this close to death.

"As far as I'm aware, she's the last." Ledger ran his hand through his hair while pacing beside the pond.

"How can you know that?" I dared to ask.

"Because she was my father's true mate, and she rejected him."

Preorder Moon Kissed Here!

About the Author

Lela Grayce lives in rural Wyoming in a small college town. She is married to her best friend and hero. By day she is a working mom and wife but by night she is lost in dreams, moonlight, and delusions that she is, in fact, Batman.

You can connect with me on:
f https://www.facebook.com/LelaGrayce

Subscribe to my newsletter:
✉ https://www.subscribepage.com/lelagrayce2023

Also by Lela Grayce

Ashes of Blood: Dragon Mafia Chronicles Book One
Do not serve drinks to a dragon mob boss. They bite. Zero stars. Do not recommend.

Blood Arrow: The Forest Hood Series Book One
There's safety in the forest.

Arrow of Loxley isn't the simpering lady of court she pretends to be.

Witch's Fancy: Watchers and Artifacts Book One
Despite owning a magic shop, having to play it safe by keeping a low profile on her talents has caused Fancy's life to fall short of the mystical adventure she hoped for. Until a detective from the Nightwatch sauntered in. Detective Walker is as hot as they come and has a powerful need... for Fancy's unique abilities.

Crimson Horizon (Blood of the Sea Book One)
Even monsters can have human faces...

When Lavinia Maycott's home is attacked by villainous pirates, she isn't sure how to find peace being a survivor. With her family murdered, she has only one place to go. However, her betrothed's estate isn't the safe haven she was expecting.

Areion (Lunar Medallion Series Book One)
Twins raised far from the darkness are the key to Gaai's salvation.

Turning eighteen is the highlight of every teenager's life. Or at least it is for Wendy and her twin sister DeeDee. When their adoptive parents gift them with medallions belonging to their late mother, they have no idea their lives are about to change.

Made in the USA
Middletown, DE
26 September 2023

39027241R00073